PRAISE FOR

BRAVE MEN RUN

A NOVEL OF THE SOVEREIGN ERA

MATTHEW WAYNE SELZNICK

"The brilliance of *Brave Men Run* is not only in its vision, but its execution. Matthew Wayne Selznick spins a superhero story that transcends predictable 'grim-n-gritty' and 'rock-'em-sock-'em' conventions, capturing a realism and emotion rarely seen in the genre. Part Stan Lee, part John Hughes, *Brave Men Run* will make you believe, once and for all, that a man really can fly."

—J.C. Hutchins, author of *7th Son*

"Selznick has effortlessly spun a strong nostalgia for the '80s with a fascinating alternate history where the superpowers wake up and may not be entirely hip on the idea of serving the rest of mankind. If Peter Parker had been one of the characters in 'The Breakfast Club', you would have *Brave Men Run*."

—Mur Lafferty, Parsec Award-winning author of *Playing For Keeps*

"A great read, a real page turner. This book could be a bestseller."

—Henry Baum, author of *North of Sunset*

"Well written, with great dialogue... utterly convincing."

—Paul S. Jenkins, Rev-Up Review

"Amazingly good… I'm totally hooked! Matthew's prose is clean and true…"

—Jesse Willis, SFFaudio.com

"This book rocks. It's engaging, the characters are robust… You won't be disappointed."

—Evo Terra, author of *Podcasting For Dummies* and founder of Podiobooks.com

"I thoroughly enjoyed *Brave Men Run* for its sympathetic characters, its eighties nostalgia, and its comic industry in-jokes, as well as its thoroughly entertaining story! If John Hughes had written the 'X-Men' films, this is what we would have gotten."

—Steven H. Wilson, Parsec Award-winning creator of *The Arbiter Chronicles*

"The '80s feel is realistic across the board, and the voice the author gives to Nate Charters… is on the mark. Children of the '80s will enjoy the references, comic book readers will enjoy the references to the 'silver age' of comics, and the story is enjoyable to boot."

—Patrick Holyfield, author of *Murder at Avedon Hill*

"Matthew Wayne Selznick has created a fascinating and imaginative world of the Sovereign Era. If you love 'Heroes' and 'X-Men,' you will love *Brave Men Run.* It will keep you turning pages until the end."

—M. H. Bonham, author of *Prophecy of Swords*

"A fantastical novel written with that all-too-rare attention to character and drama… Selznick speaks softly—yet eloquently—and wields a very big literary stick."

—Mark Jeffrey, Ulysses Award-winning author of *The Max Quick* Series

BRAVE MEN RUN

A NOVEL OF THE SOVEREIGN ERA

MATTHEW WAYNE SELZNICK

A SWARM PRESS book
published by arrangement with the author

ISBN-10: 1-934861-09-X
ISBN-13: 978-1-934861-09-7
Library of Congress Control Number: 2008927521

Swarm Press is an imprint of Permuted Press (permutedpress.com).

This book is a work of fiction. People, places, events, and situations are the product of the author's imagination. Any resemblance to actual persons, living or dead, or historical events, is purely coincidental.

Copyright © 2006 Matthew Wayne Selznick
All Rights Reserved.

Cover art by Jared Axelrod.
Title design by D.L. Snell.
Copy edited by Leah Clarke.

No part of this book may be reproduced, stored in a retrieval system, or transmitted by any means without the written permission of the author and publisher.

10 9 8 7 6 5 4 3 2 1

This work is licensed under a Creative Commons Developing Nations 2.0 License

You are free:

- to Share - to copy, distribute and transmit the work
- to Remix - to adapt the work

Under the following conditions:

- Developing Nations. You may exercise the above freedoms in developing nations only.
- Attribution. You must attribute the work in the manner specified by the author or licensor (but not in any way that suggests that they endorse you or your use of the work).

For any reuse or distribution, you must make clear to others the license terms of this work, as found here: http://creativecommons.org/licenses/devnations/2.0/

Any of the above conditions can be waived if you get permission from the copyright holder: http://www.mattselznick.com

Dedication

For Ray, Stan, Steve, and Jack... with thanks.
For Dee, for all she endures.
&
For all the folks who listened.

ONE

I was used to eating alone.

I mean, I preferred it. When I'm hungry, I need a lot of food. I really put it away, and it's easier if I can just concentrate on getting fuel in me without having to pay attention to my friends.

Not that there are whole lot of friends to distract me in the first place. We're talking, like, count-on-one-hand quantities, here. We're the misfits, rejected by all the other cliques at Abbeque Valley High, too weird for the rest, and even in my little band of weirdoes, I stand out.

So it's just as well that Abbeque Valley's gotten so crowded over the last few years they have two lunch periods, and my friends happen to have the other one. I can concentrate on eating.

On the eighteenth of April, 1985, I sat down in my usual spot in the commons, against the wall of Ms. Elp's office, and got to it.

Yes, it was *that* day. It was a Thursday, kind of on the cool side. Do you remember where you were and what you were doing?

Anyway, I liked to sit against Ms. Elp's wall because she had a big window, and she spent her lunch looking out at the commons, keeping an eye on things. She's the discipline advisor—if you're going to get busted, you'll deal with her. For a freak like me, having her literally at my back was a little insurance I'd be able to eat my lunch in peace.

It's not always enough.

My hearing is very, very sensitive. Even with the racket of a few hundred kids yammering away while they eat their lunches, I can pick out certain things that might be important to my well-being. It's part of what makes me different, same as needing to eat so much so often.

I was halfway through my second salami sandwich when I heard the distinctive, sloshing whoosh of a partially open carton of milk flying through the air. It's a sound I've heard before, and I've learned from the past.

I grabbed my lunch bag in one hand, my backpack in the other, and stood up. I moved a few feet to the left.

The milk bomb burst against the wall. Pretty good shot. My back had been there a few seconds ago.

I looked across the commons along the arc of the milk bomb's trajectory. I was not surprised to see Byron Teslowski standing over in the jocks' corner, holding court with his Wing-men. I was a target for a lot of jerks, but I've had Teslowski's special attention since sixth grade.

What did get me was the look on Teslowski's face. He didn't have his customary grinning sneer going.

He looked disappointed, and confused, sure, but there was something else there I couldn't figure out. We locked eyes for a second before Terrance Felder knocked him on his arm and got his attention, and that was that.

I sighed. Milk dripped down the wall, and pooled at my feet. I was still hungry. Ms. Elp, who somehow missed the whole thing, caught my eye through the window and gave me a curt smile. I could see myself in the dim reflection of the window: short brown hair that seemed to shed instead of ever needing to be cut; green eyes that were way too big for my face.

I looked away.

A pack of girls strolled by. The alpha bimbette, Gaby Samson, had been wearing spandex tops and leggings since "Flashdance" came out. I tried not to notice how puberty had so recently blessed her. She took a second to look me up and down.

"Nice puddle," she said. They all laughed, musical and thrilled with themselves.

Just about your normal day for Nate Charters, boy freak.

TWO

I managed to get through the next three periods without incident. Seventh period, last of the day, was a study hall for me. I don't know if anyone actually spent that time studying. The ones old enough to drive usually just went home. Abbeque Valley was a closed campus, but even Ms. Elp looked the other way when it came to the mobile students.

I was a sophomore, not quite sixteen, and still dependent on the school bus. So was my best friend, Mel Wilson. Seventh period was a time for us to debrief one another on the mishaps of the day. He met me on the stairs that led down to the athletic field.

"Anything to report, Mr. Charters?"

"Byron Teslowski tried to milk-bomb me at lunch."

Mel stroked the few dark whiskers he'd coaxed out of his chin. "Testosteronski ought to know better by now, I think."

We started down the stairs. "He does." I thought about the odd look on Teslowski's face. "I know he does..."

Teslowski had been harassing me long enough to be familiar with the fringe benefits that go with my wacky metabolism and Japanese-cartoon facial features. He should have known I would hear the milk bomb, just like I could smell his crappy cologne from fifty paces. Just like I could out-run and out-jump any kid in school, if I wanted to.

Never stopped him from hassling me. I guess it never stopped me from letting him hassle me, either.

"So what's the point?" Mel said.

"I don't know. Sport." I frowned. I was missing something, I knew it. "What about you?"

"Claire's got an Open Door, if we want to go hang out."

Mel's friend Claire was a Drama geek who lived in the tract homes just beyond the athletic field's fence. Since a lot of us had seventh period free, she let us hang out at her place until the buses came. Open Door. It beat sticking around at school.

"Who's gonna be there?"

"I think Jason, and of course Greg Fonseca. Some friend of Claire's I don't know—Rita or Lita or something."

Jason Talbot was part of our little misfit band. Greg Fonseca, who wanted to have sex with Claire, was neutral. "Okay."

We were at the bottom of the stairs. To the left, unfortunates with seventh period Physical Education class were doing calisthenics on the blacktop under Coach Zick's narrow gaze. To the right were the pre-fab classrooms and the upper parking lot. Straight ahead were the athletic field, and the little hole in the fence that led to Claire's neighborhood.

I sighed and adjusted the backpack on my shoulder. It would be a long walk, out in the open, exposed to enemy eyes. Mel and I exchanged glances, tight-lipped.

"Once more into the breach," he said.

We headed out at a rapid clip, looking ahead. The further we got from the main building of the school, the more I felt like I was being pushed by the threat of discovery. At any time, Ms. Elp could appear at the top the stairs, spot us, and haul us back to her office. Every step across the short grass of the athletic field increased our chances of a clean escape.

Unfortunately, the further into the athletic field we got, the bigger the chance we would be seen by the kids doing P.E.

Mel and I were used to their taunts, but when the "faggots," and "gayboys" came, we picked up our pace even more. I don't know why every other guy in school could have a best friend—any friend, for that matter—but if I did, I must be gay. I knew I could partially blame my negative rep on Teslowski's years of badgering. One day I'd thank him.

I kept my eyes on the fence. We were nearly there when Mel looked over his shoulder.

"Oop." He looked back quickly.

"What?"

"Ms. Elp is looking at us."

I risked a glance. I saw her at the top of the stairs. My eyesight's as good as my hearing. I could make out every color in the tartan pattern on her long skirt, but I knew we were too far for her to know our faces.

"We're cool," I said. "We're too far away."

"What if she asks us where we were, tomorrow?"

I shrugged. "Think of something. Plausible deniability, you know?"

"Hm."

We made it to the gate and slipped through. Stepping on to the quiet late afternoon street was like casting off irons. I shifted the backpack on my shoulder and tilted my head.

"Claire's already got things started, sounds like."

"What do you mean?"

"I can hear her stereo."

Mel grinned. "Let me guess. Berlin?"

"Good guess, but no… it's…" I gave it a second. "It's Duran Duran."

"I was gonna say Duran Duran!"

THREE

At Claire's, everyone was gathered in the living room. If I knew Jason Talbot, Duran Duran wouldn't be blasting from Claire's parents' big speakers much longer. He flipped through a box of records and looked up when Mel and I let ourselves in.

"Dude! She's got, like, all three "Synchronicity" covers!"

Greg Fonseca, slouched on the couch like he didn't care about anything, least of all Claire, muttered, "There's five covers."

Jason slid the vinyl from one of them. "Well, she's got three." He stood up to switch records and nodded a greeting to us. "What's up, dude?"

"Nada," I said. Mel and Jason clasped hands, their arms making a "w."

Claire came out from the back of the house. Fonseca sat up straight and smiled at her.

"Hey, guys!" Claire bounced with enthusiasm when she wasn't putting on a Molly Ringwald pout.

It was while we were saying our hellos that I caught the scent. Baby powder and new sweat, plus the mysterious undertone of female pheromones. It absolutely wasn't Claire. She had never, ever smelled like this. I looked around, confused and enthralled.

Then I saw her, coming down the hall. She was tall, with a shock of blonde hair done short and curly on top of her head—

more Madonna than New Romantic. She had hazel eyes and a wide, smiling mouth and the smell of her was making me dizzy.

Claire introduced her. "Everybody, this is my friend Lina. Lina, everybody."

I don't know what else was going on in the room. I only know that Lina walked directly up to me and stuck out her hand.

"You have the most beautiful eyes."

I don't remember taking her hand. I was too caught up in the way her own eyes sparkled, and the way she managed to never lose the smile on her face the whole time she looked at me.

And she kept looking at me.

I'm used to the uncomfortable, curious stares people send my way. I'm noticeable. I'm different. I know it. This wasn't that kind of look. No one had ever looked at me the way she did.

I was suddenly aware of the lack of conversation in the room. The only sound was from the stereo: Sting's hollow tenor crooned "Walking in Your Footsteps" again and again. Claire finally spoke.

"Yeah... um, okay, then. Lina, this is Nate."

I think I smiled. My lips felt like someone threw wet pasta on my face.

"No one's ever told me that before," I said. I silently thanked God my voice didn't crack.

"That makes me special," she said. "I'm Lina Porter."

"Nate Charters." I finally noticed we were shaking hands, very proper. We both laughed about it at the same time, let go, and the moment passed.

My friends moved in.

"I'm Jason." Lina nodded at him and smiled.

"Claire's friend from O'Neil High!" Mel tipped an imaginary hat. "Nice to finally meet you."

"Likewise. But I'm not so much at O'Neil now." She gave Claire a celebratory wink. "I'm doing home study, as of last month."

Claire said, "Lucky!"

Fonseca gave Lina a quick nod and turned his attention to Claire. "Hey, what are you doing tomorrow night, anyway?"

Claire cocked an eyebrow in his direction. "I'll think of something," she said with a laugh. She grabbed Lina by the arm and steered her back down the hall. "C'mere, you!"

They giggled their way to Claire's bedroom and disappeared behind the closed door. I took a few steps down the hall. If I could put just a little distance between me and the volume of the stereo, I might be able to hear their conversation. I wasn't really big on spying on people, but I had to know if they were talking about me…

My friends had other ideas.

"Dude, score!" Jason punched me on the arm.

"It would seem you have a new friend, Nathan," Mel put in.

Automatically, I rubbed my arm for show. Jason would have to try pretty hard to hurt me, but over the years I'd learned to downplay my so-called gifts. I didn't want to call any more attention to myself than I had to.

"What? You think so? Why?"

On the couch, Fonseca shook his head.

Jason rolled his eyes. "Dude, she was, totally, like, staring at you!"

"And in a good way." Mel smiled slyly. "Probably why you didn't realize it."

I tried to frown at him, but it didn't get through the goofy grin on my face. "You think?"

Fonseca huffed. "Dude, whatever!"

" 'S'matter, Greg," Jason jabbed, "don't like someone else getting the attention?"

"Seriously," Mel said. "At least it's not Claire giving Nate the eye!"

Fonseca finally got off the couch. "Whatever," he mumbled. We looked at him. Now that he was up, he had to do something. He dived for Claire's record box and picked one out.

The chiming keyboards and "Hey, hey, hey, heys" of Simple Minds' "Don't You Forget About Me" rang forth. Claire burst back into the living room.

"I love this song! I can't hear it enough!" We would all hear it more than enough in the months that followed, but right then, it was fresh and different.

Lina came up behind her. She looked at me quickly and a smile flashed on her face. "Isn't it from that movie?"

"'The Breakfast Club.'" Claire bopped her head in time to the trotting bass line.

Mel inspected the album cover. "Right—a bunch of kids get detention together." He smiled at Jason. "Hey, it's your life story, Jase!"

"Nyuk, nyuk."

Fonseca had worked his way next to Claire. "Hey, maybe you'd wanna go see it on Friday?"

Next to me, intoxicatingly close, Lina just barely whispered, "Oh, please."

I tilted my head and said quietly to her, "He won't give up, will he?"

She turned to me, eyes wide, that toothy smile back on her face. "You weren't supposed to hear that!"

"I've got really good ears," I said.

"I'm gonna have to remember that."

Claire said, "I saw it last weekend already."

Fonseca stuck out his chest a little. "With who?"

"With my sister!" Claire rolled her eyes.

"Oh." Greg went back to the couch. "Okay."

Lina said to me, "So, have you seen it yet?"

"No…"

"Do you want to see it?"

I took the album from Mel. "Yeah, uh, I guess. It's got that kid from 'The Outsiders.'"

Mel stroked his chin-pubes. "Um, Nate, I don't think that's what she meant."

I was completely without a clue. It must have been obvious on my face.

Lina put her fists on her hips and stuck out her chin. "I want to, y'know, see it with you, Nate." She backed off a touch. "If you want to."

"Oh!" I floundered, adrift. This beautiful girl with the narcotic scent was asking me out? "You want..." I felt myself starting to redden.

"I can't."

Lina seemed to deflate. "Oh, okay, that's cool..."

Jason's mouth dropped open. "Dude..!"

"No, I mean..." I looked at Lina. "I don't have a car."

Mel made a theatrical production out of speaking to me from one side of his mouth. "Nate. She asked you out. She. Asked you."

Lina was all smiles again, and eyes only for me. Every time she looked at me, I felt lighter.

I felt normal.

"It's no problem," she said. "I can drive us."

I smiled back. "Oh. Okay."

Mel spread his arms, presenting the two of us. "There you go!"

"Is Saturday okay with you?" Lina asked me.

"Uh, yeah... yeah!"

"Good." She took a pen out of one of the pockets of her peasant dress and held it ready above the palm of her hand. "What's your number?"

Mel shouted, "Oh, shit!"

Jason gave him a look. "Dude, chill."

"What's wrong?"

"We're gonna miss the bus!"

I looked at my watch. It was way late. Even if we were on school grounds, we wouldn't have time to make the parking lot.

"Crap."

Lina had a small smile on her face. "You still take the bus? Oh, you poor dears."

Jason dug in the pockets of his stonewashed jeans and counted change. "I've got enough for the regular bus, I think."

Mel dialed down, but he looked morose. "That'll take hours."

I tried to calculate if public transportation would get me home before my mother. If not, I'd need a story to explain why I wasn't in the parking lot when the bus came.

"Hey, boys."

We all looked at Lina.

"I'll drive you home."

"Yeah?" said Jason.

"That's capital!" said Mel.

I smiled at her. "That's great."

"That way, I'll know how to get to your house Saturday night."

Somehow I had forgotten that this gorgeous girl had made a date with me not two minutes ago. "Oh, right…"

Mel put a chummy arm around Lina. "You're all right, Ms. Porter."

"My adoring public," she said. She looked right at me.

FOUR

Jason lived all the way over by Lake Abbeque. You'd never guess his parents could afford the big house, if Jason's ratty, strategically ripped wardrobe was any indication. Mel lived two blocks up from my house. For the brief time between his place and mine, Lina and I were alone in her little silver Volkswagen Golf. That was a first for me.

I mean, I've been in cars with girls who are my friends before, but none of them ever told me my eyes are nice or asked me out. The radio saved me from dorky silence the whole two blocks when Toto Coelo's "I Eat Cannibals" came on.

"Ugh!" Lina jabbed at the pre-selects on the dashboard. "I'm so tired of that stupid song!"

"I saw the video," I said. "They look like something out of 'Sigmund and the Sea Monsters.'"

"Totally."

The next two stations were running commercials. Finally, Lina found something we both hated enough to laugh about.

"Oh, man," I said.

Lina laughed, and sang along in a ridiculous bass. "I wear my su-hun glasses at night..."

I picked it up. "So I can so I can..."

The radio ruined our fun when the announcer cut in with a special bulletin.

"Aw, man," Lina turned down the volume.

"We're here, anyway," I said. "Third house on the left."

"Oh, okay."

Lina hooked into the driveway. My mother came out the front door immediately.

"Oh, hey, I'll introduce you to my mother," I said.

"She looks pissed," Lina said.

I got out of the car. My mother couldn't have been home long; she was still in her work clothes, and she likes to get comfortable as soon as she gets home.

"Where the hell have you been?"

I was startled. "I missed the bus…"

"I called the school. Ms. Elp looked in all your usual places, and you weren't there."

"Well…" I fought a minor panic that she'd called the school and I wasn't around, but I was also totally confused. Why did she need to look for me in the first place?

"I'm not late, or anything…" In fact, with Lina driving us more directly than the bus, I was a little early.

Lina leaned over and stuck her head out the passenger window. "Hello, Mrs. Charters. I'm Lina Porter."

My mother glanced at her, then glared at me. "We don't have time for your friends right now. I need you in the house."

"But…"

"Right now!"

I looked at Lina, who looked as confused as me, and a little angry. I shrugged emphatically. "I—I guess I have to go…"

"Can I still call you for Saturday?"

"Yes!" I pulled a pen out of my jeans pocket, grabbed her hand, and quickly scrawled my number on her palm. Lina beamed like it was the combination to Fort Knox.

My mother stood by the front door. I could hear the television inside, which was another oddity for a weekday afternoon. "Right now, Nathan!"

Lina backed her car out of the driveway and onto the street. I could see her watching me in the rear view mirror as she drove away.

I followed my mother into the house.

"Have you heard the news?"

"About what?"

She looked at me, her mouth slightly open, and shook her head. "That explains that." She hustled me into the living room. "Sit down."

I sat down on the couch, facing the television. She stood behind me, her hands gripping the back cushions. There was adrenaline in her perspiration, a sharp tang in my nostrils.

On television, a middle aged-man in a business suit floated over the heads of a crowd of reporters. In the background, the Washington Monument gleamed like bone.

FIVE

"What is this?"

My mother's voice was terse. "They'll show it all again. It's all that's on."

The scene switched to the same man standing on solid ground behind a lectern with the usual tangle of microphones on it. His blue eyes scanned the audience. He put his closed hand in front of his mouth, cleared his throat, and then put both hands on the lectern.

"My name is Dr. William Karl Donner. As many of you know, I made my name in the field of neurosurgery. Fewer people know that I haven't practiced in the last few years. I've directed my energies to a research institute located east of Missoula, Montana.

"The Donner Institute has come under some scrutiny lately. Because of our insistence on privacy, the Federal Bureau of Investigation is concerned that we're organizing some kind of militia up there. I have come to Washington today to meet with Attorney General Meese, and others, so that the purpose of the Institute, and my own mission, can be clarified.

"Before I meet with them, I wanted to address the American people, and by extension, the people of the world. I appreciate you all coming out here. I promised you all something remarkable. Here it is."

That's when he did it: he spread his arms and just lifted right off the ground. The picture went a little crazy while the cameraman tried to keep Donner in the frame. I guess he was caught off guard. So was everyone else; you could hear gasps and shouts from the crowd.

The picture fuzzed for a split second. Donner spoke again, a good eight feet above the microphones on the lectern. It didn't matter; somehow his voice carried.

"This is not a trick. There are no wires, no rods, and those of you watching this on television should know that the photographers and cameramen recording this are not participating in any kind of hoax."

Donner turned slowly in the air, as if he was trying to show us all there wasn't anything up his sleeve. He slowly settled back behind the lectern.

The crowd of reporters was totally silent.

"What I've just done is an inconsequential parlor trick compared to my full creative ability. I am here today to tell you that I am not the only person who possesses such unusual abilities—indeed, there are several thousand of us across the globe."

The reporters burst with flurry of questions. Donner held up his hand.

"Please. I will take a handful of questions after my statement. Allow me to continue." When he spoke, he didn't raise his voice… but he was somehow loud enough to be heard over the reporters. It made me shiver, and it was more than enough to quiet them.

"Thank you. As I said, there are thousands of us all over the world. We live among you. While we are different—some may even look different—most are almost the same as you. I can assure you that none have the kind of innate power I possess, or anything like my control… and that's why I'm here today.

"Please listen carefully.

"The major powers of the world have been aware of the existence of my people for some time. I have evidence, which I am prepared to distribute to the major media syndicates, that we are often subjected to human rights abuses such as imprisonment, torture, and even experimentation. It will be seen that the United States of America is not excluded from my claim.

"Therefore, I appear before you today not only to declare our existence. I stand today before the eyes of the world and declare that my people—all those people who possess unique abilities—are from this day forward sovereign individuals.

"If I should learn that one such as myself has encountered misfortune, harassment, or persecution, the party responsible will answer to me, be they individual, agency, or government.

"By the same token, if one of my people acts in a way contrary to the universal principles of compassion and dignity, they too will answer to me and mine.

"We are sovereign, we are separate. However, we have no desire other than to live our lives in peace, with you."

Donner glanced over his shoulder. In the blink of an eye, the Washington Monument changed color from ivory white to flat black. Later, we would learn that everything in and around the Monument, including every object in the kiosk down to the smallest paper clip, turned black as well.

Donner nodded, a grim, small smile on his lips. The narrow obelisk returned to normal.

"Please do not doubt that I have the ability to enforce these claims. Please do not test me. Aggression against my sovereign people will not be tolerated."

The microphones picked up the whine of fighter jets scrambling, high above the Capitol. Donner cast his gaze across the throng of reporters.

"I'll take your questions now."

The coverage broke away from the replay of the press conference. I looked at my mother.

"Is this guy for real?"

Her voice was flat. "He's real. All the networks are carrying this; none of them are claiming any of the others are pulling a hoax. It's real." She sighed. "He's real."

"No way…"

She came around the couch and sat down. I slid off the cushions and sat on the floor, my knees pulled up to my chin. Like the rest of the world, we watched television.

The White House made a statement decrying Donner's irresponsibility. Unconfirmed reports from Manhattan about a shadowy, winged monster were tied in with Donner's claim that he was not the only one. Channel four brought in a panel of experts, only there were no experts, not yet, so they found Carl Sagan, Richard Feynman, Ray Bradbury, and Daniel Schor. We were shown Donner's return to the Watergate Hotel, which was quickly evacuated of all other guests and surrounded by the National Guard. That meant Washington D.C. was in a state of emergency, and that meant that everyone was taking this seriously.

I suddenly realized my mother was weeping quictly. I was confused, and excitement expanded in my chest, but I didn't understand tears. I got back up on the couch next to her. "Hey, mom, it's all right…"

"Don't you see it?" She wiped her eyes with the back of her hand and sobbed a little laugh. "Do you really think they'll let this happen?"

I knew she meant the Government. Like most kids my age, I had a pretty strong distrust of Reagan. I carried around some righteous indignation about Central America, and could easily see myself drafted in a few years. Now this guy comes around, tells the world all those old comic books are coming to life, and practically dares Reagan to do something about it.

"I guess not."

"I was worried about you. I was afraid the school had kept you. That they had been told to because…"

I wasn't ready to really get behind what she was saying. I wanted to be like everybody else. I hated that I was different, I really did.

I still had to ask the question.

"Do you think I'm…"

She put her hand on my cheek. Her palm was hot and wet. "I've always been proud of your gifts. I love you, and I love what makes you different."

I hated it when she talked like that. It was hard not to pull away.

She must have sensed that. She stood up. "We're going to have to leave for a while. I'll call Gran Louise; we'll use the cabin."

My world was being rearranged on national television, my sense of who and what I was in disarray, but when I heard my mother say that, all I could think of was Lina. "We can't leave! Not now!"

She took me by the shoulders. "We can't be sure it's safe to stay right now. I'm not going to argue about it. No one is going to take you away from me."

"But I'm not like him!" I could hear myself yelling; I felt like a spectator, arguing with myself as much as with my paranoid mother. "I'm nobody! I'm just some freaky kid!"

Her face turned red. Her eyes burned. "You are not a freak." I knew she wasn't mad at me. She was scared. "Go. Pack enough for a week."

I took another look at the television. Bill Moyers and some skinny old guy were talking about the comic book ban in the fifties. An old black and white cartoon of a flying man fighting robots flashed by. It made me wonder if people would start dressing up in leotards and beating each other up, like in Jason's Japanese *Gekiga* books.

"Go," my mother repeated.

I made for my room and threw clothes into my duffel bag. I heard my mother on the phone with Gran Louise. If I'd been in the same room, I might have made out both sides of the conversation. As it was, I could tell they were arguing. When my mother's voice dropped to a frantic whisper, I knew they were conspiring. At one point, I heard my mother say, "I do not blame Andrew, Louise."

Andrew was my dad. He died right after I was born. Why would they bring him up? I decided to ask my mother about it. There would be plenty of time at the freaking cabin.

Things suddenly caught up with me. I slouched on the edge of my bed. My limbs were heavy.

It wasn't fair. This had been a really great day. Lina Porter said I have beautiful eyes.

My mother burst in. "You can sleep in the car. Come on."

I grabbed my bag and trudged behind her. "What about your job?"

"People will still be buying houses when this is over," she said. "It's not the end of the world. Not quite."

"Then why are we acting like it is?"

For a second she looked like she was going to answer me. Instead, she pushed me out the front door.

SIX

It was a two hour drive five thousand feet up the mountains to Kirby Lake. I slept the whole way. I dreamed I was running through the woods. Lina kept yelling at me to wait up, but I never saw her. Through the whole dream, I was a mountain lion, but it wasn't as cool as it sounds. The main thing running through my feline brain was fear. I felt like I was being chased. I was ashamed for running, but I couldn't stop.

The sound of the car tires on the gravel driveway of Gran Louise's cabin woke me up. My mother unlocked the front door. The place smelled like dust and pine needles. We hadn't been up here for a couple of years—not since the summer before I started high school. I wrinkled my nose.

"Can we open the windows?"

"It's almost freezing outside… maybe just for a few minutes, to air the place out." She zipped into the master bedroom, dropped off her bags, came back into the living room, and turned on the little television. It took a while to warm up.

"Put your bag in your bedroom," she said. "Come back after. There might be something new."

I went down the short hall to the same little room I'd slept in every time we'd come up here since I was six. Gran Louise told me my dad slept here when he was a little kid. Nothing had changed in the cabin since he had been here last, probably twenty years before. I used to think it was kind of neat, having his model airplanes and his old books and stuff there. I wasn't sure why the sight of my dead father's childhood things irritated me this time. I just knew I wanted the last four hours to have never happened.

Still, being there reminded me to ask my mother about her phone conversation with Gran Louise. I went back into the living room.

"Hey, mom."

"Shh. Watch." She pointed at the television.

The caption on the bottom of the screen read, "Live—New York City." A news helicopter splashed its spotlight across the rooftops. The light settled on something I couldn't believe.

These days, it's pretty commonplace, I know. But this was the first time. I bet you were freaked out, too.

There was a man on the edge of the roof. He had long, stringy hair. His shirt was off. His chest was huge; his shoulders, unnaturally broad. He had a cape on, but I couldn't see where it was attached.

Then, the cape spread out, and up, and I saw, along with the rest of the world, that it wasn't a cape at all. He had a pair of pale, pink wings growing right out of his shoulders.

He looked up at the helicopter, right into the camera. The reporter on the helicopter was saying something, but I can't remember a word of it. All I remember was the look on this guy's face. He was laughing hysterically. He pointed at the camera, waved, and gave us all the finger before he jumped right off the roof.

The camera and the spotlight kept up with him just long enough to see that he didn't fall. He flew away.

Of course I know now that he was Gary Chancellor, and that he was eventually killed by an angry mob of Norms during the Pilgrimage, a year or so later. But right then, that night, all I knew was that he was proof.

The television replayed Gary Chancellor spreading his wings. The caption now read "Sovereign of New York."

I knew I wasn't breathing right. I was gasping—shaking, too. My face was wet, but I wasn't really crying.

Sovereign.

They were giving the freaks a name, the name Donner himself had unknowingly coined.

Now there was a name for what I was. A label.

It's hard, even now, to explain how I felt about that. I hated being different. All my life, all I've ever wanted was to be like everybody else. Being different screwed up my whole life.

That's not just me whining. It's how it was.

Now, I wasn't alone, if people were painting national landmarks with their minds and flying around major cities. Now, I was a Sovereign. I was part of a group.

Only thing was, that group was making a big deal about being different. Or at least Donner was.

My mother said, "It's all right."

I sighed tremulously. "Oh yeah?"

She shook her head at the television. "It's not going to go well if they keep doing things like that." Chancellor gave the bird to the world in instant replay.

"Heh." I sighed again and forced a smile. "Um, in case you were wondering…"

"Hm?"

"I can't fly."

She didn't smile back. "Do you know how serious this is?"

"Um, like, duh, mom."

She crossed her arms on her chest. "That man—Donner—has sent the whole world into shock. There are… there are riots in most of the major cities, including Los Angeles. When the shock wears off, it's going to be worse."

"What's worse than riots?" I shook my head. "Why are people rioting? I don't…"

"There's going to be a lot of fear," she went on. "Do you know what happens when people in power get scared?"

She didn't wait for my answer, which is fine, because I knew she wasn't looking for one. She was lecturing.

"They attack, Nathan."

"How do you know?" I wasn't being snide.

"I remember Kent State… hell, I remember McCarthy, sort of."

"But that still doesn't have anything to do with us," I said. "We didn't have to high-tail it all the way up here."

"No?" She raised an eyebrow.

"No, we didn't!" I huffed. "Look, even if I am… like that guy. I'm not, like, crazy powerful, and stuff. Why would anyone care about me?"

"Don't assume," she said.

I felt like I was missing something. "I'm not in their league! I don't threaten anyone. Even if there are more people like Donner, they're gonna go after them, not me." I shrugged and looked around at the cabin. "It seems stupid to go running off to the mountains, like this is so far out of the way there aren't any cops or any…"

She stopped me cold. "We… are… not running, Nathan. Do you understand me?"

"Oh." My face was hot. "Sure, mom."

"This isn't a game."

"Then let's go home!" Right then, the only thing that linked me to anything normal was Lina Porter, and the fact that we made a date to go out on Saturday night. The idea that I might miss that frustrated me enough to defy my mother, which was something I rarely did.

"Not yet."

Something was wrong. The olfactory pathways that constantly brought information streaming into my mind carried the root on my mother's perspiration, and if she was going to dance around it, I was going to dig it out.

"You're way more freaked out that you need to be. What's going on?"

I swear, I thought for a second she was going to slap my face, and I guess I deserved it. Instead, she kind of deflated. Her eyes were red.

"You just have to trust me. You just have to go along with this for a little while."

I backed off. "How long is a little while?"

She glanced at the television. The Washington Monument went from white to black to white again. She hugged herself. "I don't know yet. We'll see."

I sighed. "Like I don't have a life, or nothing."

I wondered what Lina thought of my family, what with my mother being all rude to her. Probably made her wonder what I was really like, if my mother was such a case.

Then I remembered. Lina had to have seen the TV. By now, I could guess what she thought.

The more I thought of it, the more upset I got. It was bad enough being the freakiest kid in school. What was it going to do to my already non-existent reputation if I didn't show up at school the day after all this Sovereign stuff went down? Everyone would be talking about it, and, hey, where's that freaky Charters kid, anyway? You think maybe..?

Wonderful.

My mother took another look at the television. It was all rehashing of what had already happened.

"I'm going to bed," she said. "Wake me if anything new happens, if you're staying up."

"Okay."

I stared at the television. I switched channels, once around the dial. Everything had been pre-empted by the Sovereign story, even on public television and the Spanish networks. Turns out *Soberano* is Spanish for Sovereign.

No one really had anything new to say. It didn't matter. I soaked it in. Tomorrow, William Donner would begin talks with President Reagan. That was wild. It made me wonder if what Donner had said was true, that our government was abusing people like him, or like me, or whatever.

I was ready to believe it. It just figured.

This one show had some commentators discussing the implications of Donner's declaration on the Cold War. The "Nuclear War Clock" was moved another minute closer to midnight. The Russians and China put out independent statements denying abusive treatment of any Sovereign in their countries, but they both claimed this wasn't the same as admitting they had any Sovereign in the first place.

One commentator brought up the potential of Sovereign soldiers in the service of the Soviets. Everyone pretty much agreed the whole world would be screwed if we started fighting wars with armies like that.

It was depressing. It made me angry. Bad enough we had, like, a million nukes waiting to wipe us out. Now there were human bombs walking around. I started to understand why people were rioting.

Would people start hating me? More than they already did?

I had enough of the TV. I shut it off.

The cabin was quiet in the way that told me my mother was probably asleep. I wasn't anywhere near tired, not after sleeping in the car. Even if I hadn't napped, my bad mood gave me agitated energy.

I padded as quietly as possible into my bedroom. It was dark, but there was enough light for me to see. I have excellent night vision, another one of the little perks that made me, thanks to Donner, officially a freak. I grabbed my jacket and slid it on.

My mother's keys to the cabin were on the little counter separating the living room from the kitchen. I stuffed them into my jeans pocket and went outside.

SEVEN

The cabin was on a quiet stretch of road about a mile from Kirby Lake and the small village that surrounds it. There weren't any streetlights, and everything's all woodsy and overgrown. That night, the moon was barely a sliver in the sky, but that was plenty of light for me to see.

Once I was down the road a bit, out of sight of the cabin, I stopped and took a deep breath. The cold air was invigorating, and the scents of the forest filled me up.

I know I've mentioned, here and there, what it is that makes me different from everyone else. My fast metabolism, my big eyes, my weird, never-growing hair, and my night vision. I guess I should run it all down for you.

Basically, all of my senses, except for, I guess, touch, are way more sensitive than other people. I can hear a wider frequency range, and quieter sounds. My eyesight, like I said, is very sharp, and I can see in almost total darkness. The less light there is, the less color I can make out, but my mother says that's the same for everyone. Difference is, to me a night-light is like a lit room, but all done in gray.

Then there's my sense of smell. I remember once when I was a little kid, playing hide and seek with Mel and some other kids, I knew who was hiding in the room with me because I could track their scents. Sometimes, my sense of smell overwhelms everything else. This is bad when it's a bag of rancid garbage, but mega-great when it's something like Lina's personal scent.

Finally, I'm stronger than I look. I had a lot of tests done on me as I was growing up, and one doctor basically told me and my mom that my muscles can do more with less. The rest of my body, like my lungs and heart and blood, are hyped up to make that possible, but the cost is my metabolism. If I'm really active for a while, or if I'm too stressed out, I get tired faster than most people. Also, as I've mentioned, I need a lot of fuel to keep things moving.

My mother says I'm gifted. You might think it all sounds pretty cool, too. Thing is, I'm just different enough to get singled out. I'm not, I don't know, Sovereign enough, I guess you could say, to really do anything about it. I'd rather be just a nerd, or whatever, and still be able to at least say I'm normal. When I walk in a room, everyone knows I'm different. I can't hide it.

Still, up in these mountains, alone with the wind and the pine needles and everything all quiet, it's actually kind of nice. That deep breath I took told a big story, all carried on the air.

About seven feet away, under a pile of pine needles, a dead squirrel was decomposing. It wasn't gross or anything, just a musty, warm kind of smell. Down the road and off the left shoulder, in a little ravine, was some kind of small animal—a carnivore. I could smell the meat on its breath. Maybe a fox, or a coyote, or even a house cat?

If I closed my eyes and just breathed, I could make a map in my head of the immediate area, a map of all the life. Bring in my hypersensitive ears, and I could hear the soft crinkle of vegetation under the paws of that cat. I could make out, roughly, how tall the trees were based on the different tones of their leaves rustling up and down the trunks. Very faintly, I could hear the lake water slapping on a wooden dock, a couple of miles away.

I don't know. Maybe I imagined that part.

I stood there, I don't know how long, in the middle of the road, eyes closed, and just let myself be who I was. I stood there long enough for the crickets to relax in my presence and start chirping again. I stood there long enough to forget about the television, and William Donner, and the flying man, and even Lina Porter and my life in Abbeque Valley. I was just, like, there.

You know what felt good? I knew I was the only person in the world who could feel this hooked in to nature and stuff. Damn right I was special, and tough luck on the rest of you.

I opened my eyes. That little carnivore turned out to be a raccoon. It was on the gravel shoulder now, about ten feet away from me. It stood up on its hind legs and twitched its nose in my direction.

About the same time, we both heard a car coming. Mr. Raccoon hustled off into the brush. I strolled over to the side of the road and kept walking.

Headlights washed over me and a blocky white van went by. It swerved a little as it passed, and rounded the corner ahead. Through the trees, I could see its headlights tilt off into the woods. There was a screech, and a dull thud. I heard the whine of wheels spinning in air before the engine went dead.

The wind hit my face with the citrus tint of radiator fluid. I was irritated. So much for my moment communing with Mother Nature. I felt a little guilty about that, since it sounded like somebody just drove off the road. I went to check it out.

The van had gone into a little ditch. The back tires were a foot off the ground. The front of the van was kissing a fir tree.

I came up alongside the driver's door. "Anybody hurt?"

"God damn it!" It was a man's voice, loaded with irritation, but without pain or fear.

I looked in the driver's side window. An older guy, with receding, kinky hair, a short goatee, and glasses, fumbled with his seat belt.

The window was down. I pulled the lock up and opened the door. It seemed to me there were too many gear shifts next to his seat.

"Are you all right?"

"Yeah, dammit." He succeeded in undoing his seat belt, and had to lean an arm on the steering wheel to keep from tilting forward. He looked at me. His eyes narrowed.

"I'll be damned."

"Excuse me?" I didn't like the way he was looking at me. I've seen his expression before, on people getting ready to make fun of me. "I asked if you were all right."

"Oh, hell, kid, I'm fine." He shifted a little in the seat.

I didn't get why we were just hanging out. "So… do you want to get out of the van?"

He adjusted the glasses on his face and squinted at me. "I said I was fine. I still need your help, though. I don't have the use of my legs. I can't walk. Get it?"

I almost felt like going back to my stroll. I didn't like this guy's attitude.

"If you can't walk, how do you drive?"

He frowned, but his eyes were bright. "Not very well, apparently." He shook his head and sighed. He pointed to the extra levers between the front seats. "See these? The van is a custom job."

I got it. He could shift, or brake, or accelerate with his right hand. "Well, look, if I have to, I can carry you back to our cabin. It's just down the road…"

He put his head on the steering wheel and sighed. "Listen, it might be less embarrassing for the both of us if you just get my chair out of the back." He handed me the keys.

"Oh."

I went around to the back of the van. It was a little awkward, since the whole tail end was up off the ground. I managed to get the back doors open.

Inside the van, large pieces of wood and animal sculptures in various stages of completion were thrown around. There were bears, deer, even a griffin. There was also a wheelchair.

I muscled the chair out, figured out how to snap it open, and wheeled it around to the driver's side.

"Here you go," I said.

He slid an arm across my shoulders. He smelled of aspen and denim, and he was not light. I got him into the chair.

"Okay. Thanks." Once he was settled, he gave me another long look.

"What's your story, anyway? I knew this kid, down Glendora. He had this bone disorder, made his face all flat and broad. You got something like that?"

I was shocked. Doesn't matter how often it happens, I still get knocked over by people's blunt stupidity. Maybe this was worse, since the guy throwing stones apparently hadn't had the use of his legs for some time.

"Do you want my help or not?"

He scowled. "Already got it. You don't want to help any more, that's fine."

"Doesn't look like you need it." I wanted to leave him there, but something wasn't right.

He was grinning. He stuck out his right hand.

"Denver Colorado. That's my name, not where I was headed."

Totally confused, I automatically shook his hand. "Nate Charters."

"Charters?"

"What's your story, anyway?" I said back at him. "You one of those, whattaya call, deaf dudes?" I gave him a smarmy grin.

He smiled, and conceded with a tilt of his head. "Okay, Nate Charters. Nice to meet you."

"Sure it is."

Now he did laugh. "Relax. I didn't mean anything. Just taking your measure."

"Make a lot of friends that way?"

"Just enough," he said.

I bit my tongue. "I'm just up the street here. You can come in and call a tow truck, or something."

"That'd be neighborly of you."

EIGHT

He wheeled himself alongside me with strong, economical strokes. He continued to stare at me. I avoided looking at him.

"So you're, what, in high school?"

"Yep."

"Take a lot of ribbing?"

"Why do you ask?"

"Let me tell you something, kid. I was in tenth grade when I lost the use of my legs. Thirty years have gone by and not a day passes where at least one total stranger looks at me like I'm carrying the plague. Just because I'm not vertical."

I looked at him.

"All I'm saying is, you gotta find something that reminds you you're not any worse off than them," he said. "Maybe even better."

Advice like that, I've heard before. I know it's well-meaning, but it never fails to irritate me. "Like making wooden bears?"

His laughed boomed off the mountains. "That shit pays the rent, I guess. No, I'm talking about something in here." Inevitably, he tapped his chest.

I wanted to groan. "Here's the cabin. Let's keep it quiet; I don't want to wake up my mother."

He snickered. "Was someone out past curfew?"

I unlocked the door and held it open. "You might say that." He wheeled himself over the small step at the entryway with no trouble at all. I turned the light on and showed him the kitchen and the phone.

"I'll give Ditko over at the Gas 'n' Tackle a holler," Denver said thoughtfully. "He's the only one old man Lee trusts with the tow truck."

"Will he be awake?"

"I'll wake his ass up if he isn't!" Denver laughed, barely quieter than his bellow outside.

I flinched and padded to my mother's bedroom door. I listened, and sniffed automatically. Panic flushed through me when I realized Ditko wasn't the only one Denver was waking up. I backed away from the door as my mother opened it, clutching at her robe.

"What the hell is going on out here?"

"Mom, I…"

She pushed past me and into the kitchen. Denver Colorado said into the phone, "Well, put on your pants and get down here, then!" He saw my mother. "I gotta go, Steve." He hung up the phone. "Hello, Lucy."

My mother's face flickered between a scowl and a smile. "I'll be god damned. Denver Colorado."

Denver pivoted his chair. "It's been a long time."

"What are you doing in my kitchen, Denver?"

"Your boy." He cocked his head toward me and put oddly strong emphasis on the last word. "I ran my van off the road, and he helped me out. Very resourceful young man."

"I didn't know you were still up here."

He looked away from her, then back. "I had my reasons to come back."

I stepped forward. "How do you two know each other?"

Denver looked at my mother. "Well, that's a story for another time, I think, but I've known your parents since before they were married. We used to raise some hell up here, that's for sure."

"You knew my father?"

"Oh, sure—even before he met your mother, actually. He was a piece of work, that old spook..."

My mother said, "It's late, Denver. Maybe we can have lunch tomorrow. Catch up."

Something passed between them that I wasn't meant to see. A warning from my mother; reluctant compliance from Denver. "Well. I've still got a few before Ditko gets his act together. Unless you want me to wait on the porch..."

My mother sighed, a hand at her temple. "Of course not. I'll make some coffee—it's going to be instant, though."

"That'd be nice." Denver winked at me. I smiled, but I didn't get it. "So, what are you two doing up here, anyway? Isn't it a school night?"

I blurted it out before my mother could say a word. "My mom's afraid they're gonna come after me 'cause of that guy Donner and all this Sovereign stuff going down."

She turned from the open kitchen cabinet gave me a look that spoke of lousy times to come.

Denver's face scrunched up. "Lucy, that's the stupidest thing I've heard in a very long time. Why would you think the boy's so special?"

She scowled and looked up from filling a battered pot with water from the sink. "You know how things get, Denver."

"Yes, I sure do." He shook his head. "He's just a kid, Luce. He's no danger to anyone, and certainly not worth anyone's trouble when big fish like that guy in Washington are swimming around."

"That's what I said," I put in.

"You don't know that," my mother said.

"So, what, you're gonna keep him locked up in your mother-in-law's cabin and hope no one notices?" He snorted. "Hell, Luce, I took one look at him and damn near knocked down a tree with the van. That's not gonna work so well, is it?"

She seemed to shrink, but smiled a little. "You know it's going to get bad."

He shrugged. "It's always bad. I've never known you to run from a fight."

"We've managed to stay out of it so far, Denver."

"What fight?" I was utterly lost.

Denver rolled his eyes. "Ask the kid if he's managed to stay out of it, being the way he is all these years."

For some reason, I felt like I should defend myself. "It's cool, I can handle it."

Denver pointed at me and nodded curtly. "I rest my case."

My mother looked at me. "Honey, it's going to get worse. They've got a name to call you."

She was so not there. "Mom, they've got lots of names for me. Duh."

She looked a little hurt. "I mean it's going to be more difficult to make friends."

"I've got friends."

She was relentless, but her tone was apologetic. "I mean keep friends."

"But taking me up here, away from everybody, is like… like leaving the scene of the crime," I said. "It's going to make me stand out even more."

Denver nodded. "Precisely."

My mother glared at him. He spread his hands.

She sat down at the small table next to him. "You bastard." She shook her head and smiled slightly.

"Nice to see you, Luce. Really is."

"What have you been doing up here, Denver?"

He glanced at me and flashed a grin. "Passing the time. Feeding the, uh, animals." He chuckled, but I read nervousness I didn't understand. "Selling piece-of-crap art to tourists. Making do."

"Better than that, I'll bet."

Outside, a horn honked.

"Well, that'll be Ditko." Denver rolled away from the table. "No time for coffee, I guess."

"We'll go to breakfast tomorrow?" My mother asked.

"You mean you'll still be here?"

She let out a sigh that tricked her into a laugh. "Bastard. I'll call you in a few days."

"We're going home?" I felt like I'd walked into the middle of a movie, and now I could barely make sense of the ending. I shook Denver's hand. "I guess I'm glad I ran into you, Mister Colorado."

"Almost the other way around," he quipped. "By the way, 'Mister Colorado' sounds like I won a beauty contest. Make it Denver."

"All right, Denver."

"Don't take up wood carving, kid. It's rough on the hands."

He reached out, tapped my chest with one hard finger, and winked.

NINE

By the time we got home, it was the middle of the afternoon on Friday. The newspaper in the driveway announced "The Superman Lives" in gigantic black capital letters. After my mother insisted we listen to talk and news radio the whole drive back, I wasn't up for reading. I dropped it on the dining room table.

She came in behind me and swept it back up. "Aren't you interested?"

"I'll read it later. I'm Sovereigned out, mom."

She clicked her tongue critically. "You need to keep up," she said, but thankfully didn't push it.

"Is it all right if I use the phone?"

She looked at the paper again. Her nostrils flared. "Go ahead. I'm going to take a shower."

There were three messages on the answering machine: two from Mel, one from Lina. Mel called first, Thursday night. "Turn on the news, Nate." He called again about an hour before we got home, which would have been about when he got home from school. "Where were you today?" He was all hyper.

Lina called not ten minutes later. "Hey, so, this is a message for Nate. It's Lina. Call me if you still want to go out and stuff, okay?" And she left her number, like nothing had just turned the world upside-down in the last twenty four hours. Perfectly normal. Maybe even a little nervous.

I didn't even consider calling Mel. I dialed Lina's number and paced while her phone rang in my ear.

A man picked up. "Porters."

"Uh, hi… is Lina there?"

"Who's calling, please?" His voice was practiced, like a disk jockey or politician.

"Oh, it's… a friend of hers. Nate."

I heard the crinkling static of a receiver covered by a hand. Far beneath this, a conversation.

Then, she was there.

"Hey, Nate. Did you ditch today, or something?"

"Hi!" She made me feel like we'd already been talking, and I'd missed the first part of the conversation. "Uh, no, we had to go out of town. Kinda quickly."

"My, how mysterious," she said. "So, where'd you go?" There was something in her voice, but I couldn't figure it out. I wished I could smell her. Maybe she was just as anxious as I was?

"We have this cabin, up in Kirby Lake. My grandma's. My, uh, mom wanted to go up there."

Lina's opinion of my mother, shaped as it was by three very bad minutes in my driveway twenty four hours before, came through. "She's a spontaneous one, isn't she?"

I tried to laugh. "Yeah."

There was a little silence then, an uncomfortable gulf that confirmed she was as nervous as me.

She said, "Hey, did you see that guy on TV? Crazy, huh?"

Well, I thought, this is it. "Yeah. Pretty wild." I swallowed. "So… what do you think of all this Sovereign stuff, anyway?"

I pictured her, probably in her kitchen like I was in mine, propped against the wall or sitting in a chair. I paced and played slow jump rope with the telephone cord.

I imagined a shrug. "I don't know. It's kinda hard to believe. My dad says it's the start of a new age, that nothing's going to be the same… I can't even believe it's real."

"Yeah."

"I mean, how could anyone even do all that stuff? And we're supposed to believe a guy with gargoyle wings?"

"Well…"

"So, what are you doing Saturday night, anyway, around seven? Off on another day trip?"

I swerved and changed mental lanes to catch up with her. She made me dizzy, even on the phone. I laughed. "No day trips." I hoped. "What am I doing around Saturday night around seven?" I relaxed a little. She wouldn't be asking me out if she thought I was the anti-Christ.

"Well, 'The Breakfast Club' is at the Kane Theater at seven thirty. You still want to go, right?"

"Hold on."

I covered the receiver with my hand and hollered. "Mom! Can I go out Saturday night?"

My mother, in her around-the-house sweats, toweled her hair as she came down the hall. "You don't have to yell."

"Sorry." Lina had me so distracted, I hadn't even noticed the taint of steam and shampoo drifting through the house. "Can I go out tomorrow night?"

"With who?" Caution colored her tone.

"Lina. You met her… sort of… yesterday."

"The girl who drove you home."

"Yeah. We wanna go see 'The Breakfast Club.'"

I watched the "no" begin to gather on her face. I gathered my arguments.

"I guess so," she said. My mouth dropped open. "Just be careful… it's still…"

I twisted away from her and uncovered the phone. "I can go," I said to Lina.

"Awesome!"

"You still remember how to get here?"

"I was just there, like, yesterday, Nate."

I think I was blushing. "Right. Sorry. I guess that seems like a long time ago."

She laughed lightly. "Do you miss me, Nate?"

"I guess so..!"

We said awkward goodbyes while my mother hovered. The phone rang the instant I hung up.

It was Mel.

"Hey, you're home!"

"Yeah, we just got in."

"I know."

I looked around. From long experience, my mother knew I was talking to Mel. She went away. "You know, how?"

"Remember that telescope I got for my birthday? Turns out the angle's just right to see your driveway from my window." He sounded very proud of himself. "I saw your mom's car pull up."

I shook my head. "You need a hobby."

"Whaddaya think that is?" He adopted a conspiratorial tone. "Besides, you'll be interested to know I saw another car cruise by your house this afternoon. A car belonging to a certain tall blonde woman…"

"Lina came by? Here?" I suddenly felt very light.

"Yep."

"Why would she do that?"

"I haven't the slightest idea," Mel said. "Especially when she knows I live right up the street. Maybe she thinks you can introduce her to William Donner."

I came crashing down. I didn't say anything.

"Um, I was kidding."

"Not so funny, Mel. So you heard."

"Who hasn't heard? It's like when Reagan was shot, it's all over TV, it's all the teachers want to talk about—it's pretty cool."

"I don't know about that…"

"Mm." I knew Mel well enough to guess that he was stroking his chin-pubes. "Are you freaking out, Mister Charters?"

I sighed. "I don't know… I mean, what do you think? Is everybody… I mean… are people, like…"

Mel adopted a fatherly tone. "Look, Nate, most people don't know you're anything more than a funny looking kid. Only a few of us know about your… um…"

"Sovereign?"

"Exactly. Your Sovereign shit. The night vision and what not. And we're your friends."

"Okay. So everybody's cool?"

"It's cool." Mel chuckled. "You're still a geek, Nate, just like the rest of us. What's different, really?"

"Like, everything, if you believe my mother."

"Ah. So that's why you left town. But, why? Really?"

I cast about with my nose and ears. My mother was in the other side of the house, out of earshot. "She thinks the government's gonna come after anyone who might be a Sovereign. She thinks they'll come after me."

Mel snorted. "No offense, Nate, but I think they have more to worry about with that floating freak."

I knew Mel meant nothing by it. He had never, ever, made a derogatory comment about my differences. Now that I was member of a new minority group, casual bigotry was something I'd just have to get used to.

Freak.

My hackles rose involuntarily. My grip tightened on the receiver. I knew I wasn't pissed at Mel specifically, but he'd be a target if we stayed on the phone much longer.

"Yeah, I guess you're right. I gotta go."

"Hey, hold on, what about Lina? Did you talk to her?"

"'Breakfast Club' tomorrow night," I conceded. "I'll call you Sunday."

"Call me when you get home Saturday night," he said.

"I'll call you Sunday," I said, and hung up.

TEN

I decided to treat my date with Lina like any other night out with a friend, at least where my mother was concerned. Since she agreed to let me go, a constant flow of news and speculation on every single channel had left her sullen and irritable. Besides, if I let myself think about my first real date, I'd be a basket case.

My mother watched me from the edge of the couch. "If anything happens," she said, "if anything goes wrong, I want you to promise me you'll come home immediately. Don't worry about the movie, don't worry about your friend, just get home."

"Mom..!"

"Promise me, Nathan."

I looked at my shoes. "I promise."

"Straight home."

"Straight home," I mumbled.

"We can't be sure," she said quietly.

She must have recognized how much of a mother she was being. She cocked her head to the side and gave me an up-and-down.

"Is that what you're wearing?"

Slightly less annoying, but still mom. I was dressed in a sleeveless black tee shirt, black High Tops sneakers, and blue jeans pegged at the ankles. "What's wrong with what I'm wearing?"

The doorbell rang. "Too late," she said, but she actually smiled when she stood up.

I opened the door and there was Lina. Her hair was moussed up in a loose wave over her forehead. Her denim jacket, clanking with pins and band buttons, was slung over one shoulder. She wore an over-sized tee shirt for the artsy band Japan tucked into a tartan miniskirt, eighteen-hole Doc Marten combat boots, and a toothy smile that made me feel too big for my skin.

"Hi!"

"Hi yourself." I grinned and let her in. "Mom, this is Lina Porter. Lina, my mom."

They shook hands, and it seemed that mutual decisions had been made to ignore their less successful introduction on Thursday. "Nice to meet you, Mrs. Charters."

"I'm glad to meet you, Lina." She looked her up and down. "You look fine, Nathan."

ELEVEN

I hustled us out of there. When my mother was on the proper side of the closed front door, I said to Lina, "So, you look nice."

She smiled and looked away as we got in the car. "I didn't know what to do with my hair. I'm waiting for it to grow out."

I ran a hand through mine. "I'll admit, that's not something I worry about."

She started the car. "Well, you keep yours really short. I don't have the right kind of skull for that."

"Actually, it doesn't get any longer than this." I tried to keep any big significance out of my voice, but I watched her carefully. "Not ever."

She couldn't spare me more than a glance as she merged into the traffic on Los Gatos Parkway. "No kidding? That's kinda lucky."

Lucky?

"Well, I guess it does get a little thicker in the wintertime." I laughed, because it sounded ridiculous unless you knew it was true. Amazingly, she laughed too, and I felt a little more confident.

"So." I tapped my fingers on the dashboard. "Anything exciting happen while I was gone?"

"Oh, sure," she said. "You were only gone, like, a day." She turned the radio on and hit the seek button. Hints of songs slid in and out of static.

"That was a pretty big day," I said.

She turned to look at me. "I guess it was." Suddenly her eyes widened, and her mouth opened in delight.

"Your eyes are totally glowing right now."

I looked away quickly. "Sorry. I can't help it."

"Hey." She reached out and touched my arm, feather light. It's entirely possible an electric current entered me where she made contact. I had to contain a shudder. "It's really cool. I love it."

The radio found a station. Ronnie James Dio pulled "Holy Diver" out of his diminutive frame.

"Yeah, right."

"No, I totally mean it." She made a face at the radio. "Blaugh. Hey, behind your seat is my tape case. Be a dear and find something better than this, okay?"

Apparently the topic of my photoreflective eyes was closed for the moment. A little confused, but more than a little grateful, I reached around and pulled a battered vinyl case into my lap.

"What do you want to hear?"

"You decide. I want to know what you like."

All her tapes were New Romantic stuff. Nothing really thrilled me, but I found one I could live with and slid it into the player. Roxy Music's "Avalon" oozed out of the speakers.

Lina said, "Did you know Brian Ferry has, like, his very own island in the South Pacific or somewhere?"

I replied that I didn't. "He sure doesn't get a lot of sun, though."

She laughed. "No doubt. It's all part of that 'pasty English guy' thing."

The female vocals toward the end came around. "I always wondered if that was the same voice as the one on "Dark Side of the Moon."

She tilted her head. "Huh. Maybe. You know, Kate Bush was discovered by David Gilmore… or one of those Pink Floyd guys."

She shrugged. "I don't know. I was never that into those prog-rock tuxedo bands."

Not minding that prog-rock stuff myself, I said, "Doesn't Spandau Ballet wear tuxedos?"

She made a gun out of her right hand and shot me. "Touché. So do the Residents, for that matter." I had never heard of the Residents, so I just nodded. "So will you," she continued, "if you go to the Prom with me."

Surely, my sensitive hearing had just heard a woman in some other car, in the next lane.

"What?"

She looked like she was having a lot of fun with the expression on my face. "Oh c'mon. Don't tell me you're one of those guys who won't dance, with that slinky walk you slide around with."

I was being pummeled, right, left, and had no idea how to defend myself, or if I was even supposed to.

"Slinky… walk?"

She laughed, strong and loud. "You are so damn adorable."

She could laugh at me as much as she wanted. "Heh. Um… you're not so bad yourself. Heh."

We pulled into Belltower Plaza. It was Saturday night and the place was busy, so Lina had to park a few hundred feet away from the theater. We got out of the car and she looked at her Day-Glo Swatch watch.

"We've got some time. Buy me an ice cream!"

"Oh, okay!"

She slipped her arm through mine and we headed for the ice cream parlor. The night was sharp and cool, and bright with a complicated texture of scents—the mosaic of people, the thick wash of popcorn butter from the movie theater, a clinging hint of car exhaust, and above all else, Lina's intoxicating signature. I breathed deep. This was a little bit of all right.

Then, the wind shifted. It carried the smell of Polo cologne and male sweat. I saw the shock of blonde-white hair, the glitter of his class ring on a puffy finger, and the Varsity jacket across gorilla shoulders. The letters across his back might as well have spelled the early end to a wonderful evening.

"Teslowski," I muttered.

"What?" Lina asked.

TWELVE

Teslowski turned and his Wingmen turned with him. He saw me, and years of conditioning caused my stomach to tremble. I silently cursed him.

He walked toward me. Terrance Felder and a couple of his other Wingmen followed, but he stopped them with an upheld hand.

Everything kind of fuzzed out for me. I opened my mouth and tilted my head forward. I stood in a slight crouch, ready for flight or fight.

Naturally, Lina picked up on my tension. "Who is this guy?" Her voice carried a thread of concern.

He stood before me. He had a good six inches and probably twenty pounds over me. That, and his history of intimidation, was usually enough for me to forget my own hyper-dense musculature probably made me at least as strong as he was. Right then, though, with Lina by my side on our very first date—my very first date, dammit—fear gave way to anger.

I stood up straight.

"Teslowski."

"Uh, hey, Charters."

I couldn't ignore what my nostrils told me. Even through the haze of bad cologne, I could sense no hostility on his sweat. The way his eyes darted deferentially to Lina, the way his hands were stuffed deep into the pockets of his letterman jacket—Byron Teslowski was, at the very least, uncomfortable to face me.

I was totally thrown off.

"So, uh, what do you want..?"

He looked around for a second. "You and me…"

I mentally filled in the rest: "right here, right now!"

Not even close.

"We need to talk about something."

I sometimes hate that my mother raised me right. The first hint of détente, and I'm ready to be a total gentleman. "Well… sure, I guess…"

He looked over his shoulder. His Wingmen were watching us intently. Terrance Felder spread his arms and shrugged. When was Byron going to kick my ass, already?

Teslowski used a stage whisper. "Not now, dude. What about tomorrow, at Romita Park?"

I was suspicious despite the evidence. "You want to meet me at Romita Park."

"Just chill," he said. "I'm serious."

No doubt that he was. What the hell.

"How about two o'clock?"

He nodded. "Yeah, cool."

His friends were calling him. He nodded to me again and glanced at Lina. "Thanks," he said to her. Then he turned around and walked away.

Lina put a hand on my shoulder. "You didn't really introduce me to your buddy Flash, there."

"Huh?"

She smiled and gave my shoulder a squeeze. "Never mind. Are you all right?"

I tried to relax. "Yeah. That guy's been a major pain in my ass since, like, forever."

"What's it all about?"

"The usual schoolyard crap, I guess." I shook my head. "At least, it has been. I guess I'll find out tomorrow." I looked at her and forced a smile. My tension evaporated when she smiled back. She was magical.

"Do you still want ice cream?"

She consulted her watch. "We probably don't have time. Let's just do the movie."

"The Breakfast Club."

John Hughes had a tight lock on the teen-aged psyche. He gave us a movie of our very own. I felt the opening chords of the soundtrack physically, in my chest, and was committed from that moment.

Emilio Estevez' tortured jock character made me think about Teslowski.

The first week I knew him, we were friends. Teslowski was new to Romita Elementary, and new in town. I made friends with him. I was glad to have a chance to be a friend with anyone besides Mel. Even then, Mel and I were stranded on a sinking island in the middle of a rapidly flooding sea of abuse.

It didn't take long for the other kids to set Byron Teslowski straight: Mel and I were Not Cool. The second week, Teslowski stole my backpack and threw it against the softball backstop until the strap caught and it hung there, thirty feet up, at the very top. It set our pattern for the next few years. He became increasingly popular, and I became ever more ostracized.

Now, he had changed, just since Thursday at lunch. In the middle of the movie, I realized what I'd read in him in place of his usual bluster and arrogance.

Byron Teslowski was scared.

I couldn't believe he was afraid of me.

Curiosity had me almost looking forward to Sunday.

Almost.

Lina and I shared a bucket of popcorn. Inevitably, our hands bumped reaching in. Our fingers intertwined and stayed that way for the rest of the movie. We looked at each other. There was so much buoyant happiness in her smile, I was filled with rushing, exhilarant joy. This girl, this gorgeous, older girl, was genuinely pleased to be with me, Abbeque Valley's only genuine Sovereign freakazoid.

She thought my glowing eyes and fuzzy hair were cool.

She asked me out!

The movie ended and I felt like Judd Nelson, one hand triumphantly raised high. I glanced at Lina.

"Your face is gonna hurt," she said.

"Why?"

"You've had that goofy grin there for a while, now."

I laughed, a little giddy. "How would you know? Weren't you watching the movie?"

Caught with her hand in the cookie jar, she smiled demurely. "Sure, of course I was." She stood up and gathered her jacket and purse. "Now what?"

I shrugged and stood up. I took a moment to stretch and sigh. "I don't mind. Just don't say you're dropping me off."

She made a great show of tapping her chin with a finger and looking at the ceiling. "Hm. Let me see." She bit her lip. "No… no, I don't think I'm through with you yet."

She took my hand and led me out of the theater. "C'mon. We'll just cruise around and see what looks like fun."

My eyebrows went up. "In this town?"

The corners of her lips twitched. "Okay, then, we'll make our own fun."

Wow.

I ran out of snappy patter. "That, uh, that could be an option."

THIRTEEN

We drove up Los Gatos Boulevard a little ways, joking around and listening to the radio. I rolled down the window and stuck my head out to suck in the scents of the night air. It's something I've done since I was a kid, especially when I'm really happy.

We were coming up on an intersection. Lina said, "Hey, Rover, come on back for a minute. Left or right?"

I closed the window and exhaled. "Depends on where we want to go, I guess. Left is the Marine Base. Right is Kane Park, eventually."

Lina swerved the car to the right. Momentum slid me close to her.

"Hi there," she said, and leaned into me.

She was so warm. I straightened up like she'd jabbed me in the ribs. "So, Kane Park it is."

We ended up in an unfinished housing development not far from the park. Lina pulled over to the curb. She cut the engine, but turned the key so we'd have the radio. The DJ recommended we put on our headphones, as some sort of ceremony was about to begin.

Lina shifted in her seat to face me.

"So." She smiled. "Tell me about you, Nate Charters."

"Uh..." I was learning Lina was a very direct person. Sometimes it was charming. Right then, it made me want to shrink in my seat. "About me?"

"Sure! Like, is it just you and your mom?"

"Oh! Oh, like that." I realized I'd broken into a sweat. "Well, yeah. My dad died when I was just a baby. I think I was actually just a few days old, or something."

"What happened?"

"Some kind of accident at his work. Closed-casket bad."

"What did he do?"

"I think he was, like, a researcher, or something, y'know? Industrial stuff, I think."

"So you never even knew him?"

"Nope." It made me think about someone who did, though. Why had I never heard of Denver Colorado before Thursday, if he was such a good friend of my mom and dad's, way back when? It reminded me there were some things I wanted to ask my mother. I figured I would wait until this whole Sovereign thing died down a little.

"Wow. I'm sorry."

I shrugged. "Thanks. It's not really a big deal, though. I mean, I never knew what I was missing, you know? It's always just been me and my mom." I turned to face her. "What about your folks?"

"My dad's into politics." Lina made a face. "He's on the city council. My mother's, like, your basic society wife—she does volunteer work, takes care of my little brother, and hangs on my dad's arm at dinners and stuff."

"You get along okay with them?"

"I guess." She reached up and pulled a lock of her hair to her mouth. It was just long enough for her to nibble if she twisted the side of her mouth. This was Lina contemplating, and I added it to the growing list of things about her that made me weak.

"See, the thing is," she said, "I don't exactly fit in with his plans—my dad's idea of what his daughter should do with her life."

I had no idea what I wanted to do with my life, so this impressed me. "What's that?"

She smiled, tilted her head down, and looked at me through her lashes. "I want to be an artist." She shook her head. "I am an artist."

"Wow. Like what kind of stuff?"

"Whatever," she said. "I mean, it depends, y'know? I paint, I sketch, I do little clay thingies… whatever it's supposed to be."

"I can't wait to see something."

She grinned. "Be patient, Nathan. I'll ask you up to see my etchings one day."

I ran a hand across my face to cover my blushing, and laughed. "So, why's your dad got a problem with it?"

"It's not stable enough, I guess." She pouted. "He'd rather I go into law, or business, or something."

"Well, it's your choice, yeah?"

"Exactly! But he won't pay for college unless I'm doing something he approves of."

"Do you have to go to college to be an artist?"

She nodded and smiled. "You sound like Car. You're right, I guess. I mean, I can go all punk rock like Raymond Pettibon, and stuff, but I know I'd learn something if I went."

"Who's Car?"

"Oh, Carson and I have known each other since we were little kids. He's got this band, Jesus Horse."

I fought a little tinge of possessiveness. This stretched into a moment or two of silence. She misinterpreted it, but that was okay—I didn't really want to be jealous.

"So." She gave me a toothy smile and poked me in the shoulder. "Are you waiting for me to ask about all your, like, glowing eyes and stuff?"

She seemed so open, so willing to hear whatever it was I would lay on her, that I actually felt a kind of weight coming off of me. I sighed to expel the last of it.

"Yeah, okay." She took my hand. It was warm.

I sighed again, and smiled. "Okay. I'm just gonna, like, list them off, okay?"

"Yep."

I held up my free hand and counted. "I've got really sensitive hearing, and sense of smell, and eyesight. I can see in anything but, like, pitch black darkness. I'm stronger than I look—my bones are denser than normal, and my muscles, too."

"You're out of fingers." She tugged to free her hand, but I held on. That made her smile and look away for a second. When she brought her gaze back to me, her eyes were bright. "What else?"

"Well, um, that's it, pretty much." I shrugged. "Except that I pay for all of that with a really fast metabolism—I eat like a freakin' horse, and I burn it pretty fast. I crash when I can't fuel up, especially after I've done anything strenuous."

She squeezed my hand. "And strenuous for you is, like, a major workout for me?"

"I guess. Yeah."

She stared at me. Her smile never broke, and never got cold.

"You are full of surprises, Mister Charters."

"Heh. Yeah." I looked at our interwoven fingers. "I was pretty worried you'd be freaked out, with all this Sovereign stuff going on."

"You think you're a Sovereign?"

How could she be taking this all so easily? I was scared to look at her, but I needed to see her face.

"Would it matter?"

"Nope."

Her other hand was suddenly behind my neck.

She kissed me.

I was almost overwhelmed, literally. Her tongue was smoother than I thought it would be. Then my heightened senses, combined with all those churning teen-aged hormones, sent me down a laser-sharp point that drew everything I was into our kiss.

I don't know how long it lasted. We finally pulled apart, and the look of wide-eyed amazement on her face was surely just like mine. We went at it again. Our teeth clanged. We didn't care.

This went on for a while.

Finally, getting a decent breath became just barely more important than the demands of our libidos. We sat forehead to forehead, twisted in the front seats of her little car.

She was almost panting. "I think… I think…"

"What?" I was trying to relax, to cool it, but everything about her seemed luminous and white. The stew of our pheromones in the close air made me giddy. "What?"

Very gently, she pulled away from me and we sank into our respective seats. Her face was flushed. She closed her eyes and smiled, lazy and wide. "I think we'd better go back to talking for a few minutes." She rolled down the window, which helped clear the air and my mind.

"Yeah, maybe." I laughed, a little astounded. "Hey, Lina."

"Yes?"

"You, uh, you really know how to kiss." I almost added, as far as I knew.

She shook her head and pushed strands of hair off her face with a languid sweep of her hand. "Right back at you, hon." She giggled. "Man…."

"So… um… that was all right?"

She gave me another wide-eyed look. "Nate… you… you don't even know."

The fact of the matter was that I didn't. "Tell me."

She laughed, looked out the window, then at her lap. She crossed and uncrossed her legs in the cramped space below the steering wheel, then settled on curling them underneath.

"Let's just say…" The way she looked at me, with this mix of patience and, shock, I guess—I'd never seen that expression on any other person, exactly. "Let's just say I knew you'd be great. You've got all this intensity around you. I figured you'd be a great kisser. But…."

"But what?"

She ran a light finger down my cheek. "Let's just say you exceeded my expectations, okay?"

I laughed. I was pretty happy with myself, but especially with us. "Well, that's good, right?"

"Like I said, you don't even know."

We spent a few eternities just gazing into each other's eyes. She leaned forward and gave me a soft, lingering kiss. It was different than before. Our first kiss—my first kiss—had been like a hot wire. This was like a warm wave, or rain on a hot day. It was less physically intense and more… emotional.

That kiss filled me up.

She swept a hand down my face and cupped my jaw. "Time to get you home."

I understood. The evening was more than complete.

"I hate to admit it, but things are catching up with me. Popcorn burns fast."

She winked with wicked delight. "Well, at least I know it's not me that's putting you to sleep."

I shifted uncomfortably in my seat. "Right."

She started the car, and we drove in silence down the hill to my house. I spent a lot of time looking at her. She finally caught me, and fended off my adoration with an exasperated, "What… ?" toned with a broad, bright smile.

FOURTEEN

We pulled into my driveway.

"So. Thanks for the movie."

"Now who's got the goofy grin?"

We laughed, and kissed again. This time, it was somewhere between the laser beam and the warm rain. I was learning about a whole catalogue of variations.

"I want to see you again," she whispered. "In case it isn't obvious."

"Heh. I don't see any problem with that."

"Soon."

"Yes. Soon."

She gave me a quick smooch and playfully pushed me away. "Call me tomorrow. Let me know how your big showdown goes."

The cloud I was floating on suddenly dipped a couple of feet. "Man, I'd forgotten all about that."

"I have that affect on men."

"Totally." I opened the car door. "I'll call you tomorrow."

"G'night, Nathan."

I got out of the car and stood in the driveway until her car was out of sight.

FIFTEEN

Sunday morning, I slept in until my mother made enough noise around the house to wake me. I got out of bed and threw some water on my face.

The bathroom mirror showed me I was smiling.

"You have a girlfriend," I told my reflection. It grinned back at me.

I did a little dance on the bathroom rug.

I also had, I remembered, an appointment today.

A knot of tension tightened my stomach, but it didn't last. I had a girlfriend, an older girlfriend, who thought my eyes were beautiful and liked the way I kissed. Byron Teslowski just couldn't stand up to that.

I allowed myself one more look at confident me in the mirror before I went into the kitchen.

My mother was dressed for work. "You must have had a good time last night."

I stuck my head into the refrigerator and started gathering breakfast to hide the color rising in my face. "Sure."

"'Sure?' That's it?"

I moved five eggs to the kitchen counter and crouched down to get a pan. "C'mon, mom."

"Well, I mean, this was your very first official date with a girl, wasn't it? A mother has a right to be curious."

"We had a good time, I guess."

I could practically feel her smiling behind me. "You must have; you've barely looked at me since you woke up."

At least she wasn't asking me about Sovereign stuff. "It was a good movie."

"And good company, apparently." She slid a chair out from the kitchen table and sat down. "I've got a minute or two. Tell me about this girl."

I tried to clamp down on my broad smile and settled on subduing it a little before I turned around. "She's an artist."

She nodded. Her own smile was sly, and her eyes were bright with amusement. "That's interesting. What do her parents do?"

"Um, I think her dad's a politician. Her mom does, like, community work."

"Grant Porter is her father?" My mother raised an eyebrow. "I don't know why I didn't make that connection."

"You know him?"

She shook her head. "Not really. I've seen him at Chamber meetings."

"Oh." I dropped some butter in the pan and swirled it around.

"Nathan."

"Huh?"

"Did anything happen last night?"

There was no stopping my blushing now. I frantically tried to get the sensation of kissing Lina out of my head, but it wasn't going to happen.

My mother narrowed her eyes and her lips tilted. "That's not what I meant—but I can see something did. We'll talk about that in a minute."

Crap.

"Did anything happen because of the Sovereign story," she clarified.

Did Byron Teslowski's freaky behavior count? I decided that wasn't something she needed to know.

"No. Everything was cool."

"Are you sure?"

I clicked my tongue. "Mom, I'm sure. Nobody gave me anything more than the usual second glance." I broke the eggs into the melted butter.

"As far as you know," she said, but she stood up and looked at her watch. "I've got to go. What are you doing today?"

Cover story time. It's nice to have at least one member of the family who can't literally smell a lie. "I was gonna ride my bike up to Mel's, probably. Just hang out."

"All right. I should be back in time to figure out dinner. See you at six, all right? Maybe then you can tell me the other details of your date, Casanova."

"Okay."

She kissed me on the cheek and messed my hair until it was all going the wrong way, which bothers me to no end. I scowled and put it back, which only made her smile.

"Behave yourself." She gathered up her work stuff, and left.

I finished making breakfast, and set to fueling up. Lina was still on my mind, but somehow my mother had drained some of my confidence. She treated my whole thing with Lina like it was all just so cute.

It made me feel like a kid. Which is exactly how I felt every time Byron Teslowski tried shit with me: like I was ten years old.

I finished breakfast quickly, cleaned up, and remembered I told Mel I would call him today.

He answered quickly.

"Hey, Nate!"

"Hey."

"So?"

"So, what, Mel?" I laughed at how it was okay for Mel to dig at me about Lina, but not my mother. He had best friend privileges.

"So, how was 'The Breakfast Club?'"

I knew Mel wasn't interested in the movie, so much.

"Really, really great," I said, and laughed again.

He chuckled. "Cool. You guys hit it off, then?"

"Oh yeah."

The interest in Mel's tone ratcheted up. "No kidding?"

The face-stretching smile was back, and I knew he could hear it in my voice. "We drove up near Kane Park for a while, after."

"I see!" Mel didn't have a girlfriend, at least right now. He was working on one of Claire's friends.

"Yeah." I took a second to relive it. "She's pretty fucking awesome, Mel."

"Thought so."

"One weird thing, though."

"What."

I told him about Teslowski, and my pending meeting with him.

"Um, are you sure it's a good idea to go up there by yourself?"

"Mel, this is me."

Mel snorted. "And by that, you mean the kid Teslowski has tortured for the last, I dunno, forever?"

Episodes from that history flashed in my mind, and my stomach clenched until those ugly memories were replaced by William Donner floating above the television cameras.

"By that," I said, "I mean the kid who could kick his ass if he wanted to."

I almost believed it.

Mel said, "It's about time. You want me to come up there, anyway?"

I shook my head. "No, thanks, man. I don't even think it's gonna be that kind of thing. I'll come by your place after, fill you in."

"Okay. Later."

"Late."

I hung up the phone. I needed to take a shower, have some fruit, and then it would be time to go.

SIXTEEN

I got to Romita Park about twenty minutes before two. I rode my bike up and down the winding concrete paths, past the three little playgrounds and the picnic tables. No one else was there.

Romita Park bordered the playground field of Romita Elementary, with a little hillock between them. I sat on my bike and spent some time looking at the school's softball backstop; I thought about climbing all the way to the top to get my backpack, years ago.

Byron Teslowski had been picking on me, stealing my friends, and destroying my reputation for five years. A third of my life! I was surprised I wasn't more nervous that we'd be meeting, alone, in a few minutes. After last night, and Lina, it was hard to be anything other than wildly confident— especially since Teslowski acted so weird last night.

I rode back to the middle of the park and leaned my bike against a picnic table. I leapt on top of the picnic table with the same effort most folks use to step onto a curb, and smiled. I knew I was strong… the only reason people like Byron could keep me down was my own stupid lack of confidence. I hated having attention drawn to me, hated the way people looked at me, hated being called a freak.

Lina put a whole new perspective on that. Lina, and William Donner. Let Teslowski try something. Let him.

I smelled his cologne and saw him coming up the steps from the street. I debated walking to meet him, and decided he could come to me.

He wore his regular uniform: tight blue jeans, a pale blue Polo shirt, and his Varsity jacket. His spiky blonde hair was tucked under an Angels baseball cap. He saw me and walked over, hands in the pockets of his jacket.

"Hey," he said.

I looked down at him from on top of the picnic table. "Hey."

"What're you doing, standing up there?"

I squatted down. "Nothing." He probably thought I looked like an idiot up there, and I knew I probably looked like one. "So. What did you want, anyway?"

He looked to his right, toward the school. "Just talk, I guess."

"What about?" I couldn't stop thinking about the backstop, the name calling, the milk bombs, and all the other times this jock had humiliated me. I was losing my patience.

"Well," he squinted up at me. "You know that stuff that's been on TV…"

"Who doesn't? What about it?"

"'Sovereign,'" he said. "You think that's you?"

I stood up again. "What do you care?"

He threw his hands into the air suddenly. "Fuck, dude, don't be so defensive!"

"It's you, Teslowski," I snapped. "What am I supposed to be?"

He looked everywhere but at me. "Yeah," he mumbled. "Sorry about that."

I didn't trust my own hypersensitive ears. "What did you say?"

He looked at his designer sneakers. "I said I was sorry. I'm not gonna be doing that stuff any more."

"You're not?"

"No."

"Thursday, you tried to peg me with a milk bomb."

"Dude, it missed—like you knew it was coming."

"I did. I heard it." I crossed my arms, smug.

I expected him to look surprised. Instead, he just nodded. "Yeah. I figured. I always knew there had to be more to you than just lookin' funny."

"Fuck you."

He sighed. I saw his Adam's apple move, and he looked like he didn't like what he just had to swallow. "Sorry. But you do look different from everybody. You always have."

That was the second time I ever heard Byron Teslowski apologize, and it hadn't even been a minute since the first time. It was enough to relax me some. I sat down on the edge of the table, which brought us to just about eye level.

"So, what's your point?"

He scratched behind his ear. "I was wondering. What can you do?"

"Huh?"

"I mean, like with the milk bomb. What else?"

"Why?"

"I just want to know, okay? No strings."

"No strings." I didn't completely believe him, but what the hell. He apologized.

"You have a cat?"

"Uh, yeah."

I said, "Everything your cat can do, I can do."

He squinted, snorted. "What, like land on your feet all the time?"

I looked at him.

"Oh." I watched him think it over. "Dude… that's boss!"

"Whatever." Lina sure thought it was, but I told myself I didn't care what this idiot thought.

He took off his hat and ran a hand through his hair. "So, if you're like that, how come you never tried out for any sports or nothin'?"

"I didn't like the crowd."

He got that one right away. "Oh. Yeah, right."

We were both quiet for a minute.

"So," I said, "why did you want to know all this stuff? Why have us meet here?"

"Well..." He stepped closer to me. His eyes darted around like he expected the Candid Camera crew to leap out of the bushes.

"I think I'm one of you."

Before I had a chance to digest that bombshell, Terrance Felder and the rest of Teslowski's Wingmen came up into the park.

"Kick his ass, Byron!"

Teslowski's eyes widened. "What are you guys doing here?"

Felder cracked his knuckles as he sauntered up. "We saw your car, thought we'd see what was up." He sneered at me. "Looks like we were just in time."

I slid off the picnic table and stepped sideways to get some space behind me. "You're a real shithead, Teslowski."

"I didn't..."

Felder scowled. "What's the deal, Byron? Get on with it!"

Maybe it was my night with Lina. Maybe it was William Donner turning the Washington Monument into a negative. Maybe I was pissed at myself for actually starting to believe Byron Teslowski. I was done with backing down.

"Yeah, Byron." I spat at his feet. "Get on with it."

He came up with a lie. "Dude, I didn't even know you were gonna be here."

"Bullshit. You asked me to be here, and unless it was for a date, let's go!"

Terrance Felder and the rest of the Wingmen were shocked into silence. I had never, ever, stood up to Teslowski before. It was a new world, after all. One where I didn't run.

Teslowski mouthed, "Shut up," and shook his head at me.

I took a step toward him.

"You're a pussy," I said.

His buddies howled. Teslowski reddened. He shrugged off his jacket and tossed it in Felder's direction. I heard him catch it.

Teslowski made fists. "Whatever, dude."

The Wingmen made a circle around us. I waited.

Teslowski started bobbing. "Put 'em up, Charters."

I kept my hands at my sides, fingers slightly curled. The hooting taunts of the Wingmen faded as I seemed to automatically focus in on the sound of Teslowski's breathing.

In the distance, Terrance Felder said, "Just hit him, Byron!" I hated that pudgy bastard more than Teslowski, right then.

After years of limiting himself to psychological torture, Byron Teslowski finally took a swing at me.

He was so slow. I watched his fist slip past me, darted in, and struck at his ribs with my fingers.

I didn't know what I was doing. I didn't know how to fight. I just did what felt right.

He grunted and backed off. He shot me another reluctant look, but I shook my head. I was tired of being the loser.

The smell of his sweat made me hungry.

"Suit yourself," he said. This time, he came at me with a combination, left and right, and he was faster. I twisted away, but there was no opportunity to strike back.

One of the Wingmen barked, "Stop squirming, freak!"

That word stole my restraint. I surprised Teslowski by leaping at him. We hit the grass and rolled. His fists registered as dull thuds I couldn't feel. I jammed one hand under his ribs and swiped.

He gasped, and his fear bloomed in my nostrils. I swung for his face, but he blocked me with a forearm and pushed me off with his other hand.

It was my turn to be surprised. I was in the air! Contrary to his earlier assessment, I didn't land on my feet, but hard on my right side. I actually slid a few feet before scrambling to my hands and knees.

Teslowski had a hand under his shirt. "Stay away from me!" His voice cracked. The front of his shirt grew a dark, wet stain.

Terrance Felder cried foul. "Fucker's got a knife!"

I looked at Felder. I smiled, and the skin on my face felt tight and dry. I held my hands out for him to see: empty.

The fingers on my right hand were red and sticky.

Teslowski pulled his hand out from under his shirt. He looked at the blood on his own fingers—his blood—and winced.

"You shouldn't have, dude."

At the time, I couldn't hear the real regret in his voice.

The speed with which he leapt at me was as fast as anything I could do. He slammed into me like he was sacking a quarterback. The wind left my lungs. His fists moved faster than they should have. My lip burst, wet and hot.

I panicked. I'm not sure how it happened, but we were apart again. I was on my hands and knees. Dazed, I stared at the blood from my face as it dotted the grass. I looked at Teslowski. He was on his back, clutching his crotch. His Polo shirt was glossy and red.

The Wingmen rushed to his aid. They helped him up.

Terrance Felder glared at me. "You're dead, dude."

I looked at Teslowski, and our eyes met. We both got it.

This fight was over.

SEVENTEEN

The short bike ride from Romita Park to Mel's house was zero fun. My lip throbbed. My ribs ached. My side burned where I'd slid across the grass.

What the hell had just happened?

The driveway of Mel's house was empty, but you didn't need my hearing to hear the Psychedelic Furs blasting from Mel's upstairs bedroom window. I leaned my bike against the side of the house and pounded on the front door.

I avoided using my right hand. Teslowski's blood was dry and tacky.

Mel apparently didn't hear me until the silence of the empty groove between two songs. He opened the door before the first verse of "Here Come Cowboys" was over.

Mel took one look at me and paled, which was a little scary. How did I look?

"Holy shit, Nate!"

I talked around my swollen lip. "Anyone else home?"

"No—my folks took Hermione to the mall."

I stepped into the living room and leaned against the wall. "Ice."

"Right."

I followed Mel into the kitchen, where he rolled some ice cubes in a couple of paper towels. I held them to my lips and closed my eyes.

"What the hell happened?"

If I'd been in better shape, the extent to which Mel was freaking out would have been funny. I just held up my hand for him to wait.

"Jesus Christ!"

I opened my eyes. Mel stared at my blood-stained hand, then looked rapidly around the room with perfect paranoia.

"C'mon. My room. If my parents came home and saw you like this…"

I followed him upstairs. My ribs ached with every step, and I allowed myself to wonder if they were broken. The thought made me sick to my stomach, since broken ribs meant a doctor. If my mother found out about this whole mess, I'd never be allowed to leave the house.

In Mel's room, he brushed clothes off of his bed and I sat down. Mel stared at me.

I pulled the ice off my lip and said, "Teslowski."

Mel darkened. "I figured. Son of a bitch. He jump you?"

I shook my head, which made my lip hurt. I touched it with my tongue, which made it hurt. Since I couldn't avoid the pain, I gave in and told Mel the whole incident.

"So… you cut him with your bare hands?" Mel didn't look at me.

"I guess I should clip my nails." I tried a laugh.

Mel snorted. "Probably need wire cutters." He crossed his arms on his chest and tilted his head. "You think he was telling the truth?"

The ice was pretty much worthless at that point, so I tossed the soggy, bloody mess into Mel's waste basket.

"About not wanting to fight?" I frowned; it hurt; I stopped. "Yeah. I practically forced him into it, which was not the brightest thing."

"I mean about the other thing," Mel said. "He said he thought he was a Sovereign."

"Yeah. That too." I thought about it. "When we started fighting, he was, like, slow, like any norm…" I cut that off. "Like anybody. But he got faster, real quick, and stronger, too." I shook my head. "When he pushed me off him, it was like I was flying." I indicated my broken lip. "By the time he did this, he was at least as strong as I am—maybe more."

Mel whistled. "No wonder."

I shrugged, confused.

"No wonder he's such a jock," he said. "Testosteronski's a Sovereign, but he's like, super-jock, or something. How else could he be so damn good at everything involving a ball of some kind?"

Not to mention track, and swimming, and wrestling… he'd been involved with, and excelled at, every kind of sport they offered since junior high.

"Super jock. Great."

Mel smiled. "And you, my friend, kicked his super-jock ass."

"Sure—and I'm not exactly all fucked up, here, myself." I sighed; it hurt. I stopped. "It was a draw. Plus, don't forget he didn't really want to fight me."

I had, though. I felt like an idiot. "I'm gonna have to talk to him."

Mel nodded. "Yeah, huh." He cringed as I leaned back on the bed. "Hey, Nate, your hand…"

I jerked upright before I could think about how that would hurt my side. Wincing, I said, "Sorry. I'll wash up."

Mel scooped a U2 concert shirt off the floor. "Here. Your shirt's a mess." He tossed it at me.

"Thanks." I caught it with my cleaner hand and went into the bathroom across the hall from his room.

I got my first look at my lip in the bathroom mirror. It wasn't nearly as bad as it felt. I could have laughed, but for the thought of what I had done to him. I realized I had no idea how deeply I cut him.

It made me sick. I barely made it to the toilet.

Throwing up drained me in more ways than the obvious. Adrenaline had brought me far, but my metabolism would allow no more. I was exhausted.

I flushed the remains of breakfast, washed my hands and face of blood, changed into Mel's shirt, and stumbled back to his bedroom.

He raised an eyebrow. "You gonna be alright?"

"I'm whipped."

He knew how I worked. "Crash for a while. I'll be downstairs."

"Thanks." I fell back on the bed and was out in no time.

I woke when something touched my face. I opened my eyes and saw Lina hovering above me, face scrunched and squeamish.

"Yikes, sorry..!"

I sat up on Mel's bed. My side felt a little better, and the sight of Lina was enough to almost ignore the pain in my lip.

"Hi!"

"Hi, yourself." She took my chin in her hand and moved my head left and right. "You gonna live?"

"You should see the other guy," I said with no humor whatsoever.

Behind Lina, Mel said, "I told her all about it."

"I came over to see if there was anything I could do for my tough-guy boyfriend." Lina somehow conveyed her general disapproval with a thin smile.

"Boyfriend?"

Mel and Lina exchanged a glance. Mel pointed his index finger at his temple. "Shell shock," he stage-whispered to Lina.

"Bite me, Mel." My eyes fell on the clock on Mel's nightstand. "Shit. Tell me it's not six thirty."

Mel scratched his head. "Actually, it's only six fifteen. I set it ahead so I'm never late."

Mel was always late. "That's still too late. My mother's going to kill me."

"When did you say you'd be home?" Lina asked.

"Fifteen minutes ago, Mel Standard Time." I stretched carefully to test my ribs. I decided they weren't broken.

Lina acquired a pout. "Can't you call her and let her know you're over here?"

Mel handed me his phone, and I dialed.

"Hello?" My mother's voice was clipped and abrupt.

"It's me."

"You're late."

"I know—sorry. I'm over at Mel's. Is it okay if I hang out over here a while longer?"

My mother's new paranoia welled in her voice. "I don't know…"

"We're just hanging out—we won't go anywhere." I rolled my eyes in Lina and Mel's direction.

"It's a school night," my mother said. "How late were you thinking?"

"I dunno, like, nine, I guess."

"You have your bike?"

"Yeah."

"Well, I'm not sure I want you riding home in the dark."

"Um, hello, mom, I can, like, see in the dark?"

"I am very aware of that," she said with exaggerated patience. I wondered if I pushed my luck. "Maniacs in their cars can't, though, can they?"

"Lina's here. She can drive me back."

"Oh!" Her tone changed immediately, but I wasn't sure I liked it any better. "So that's how it is!"

"So, is it cool?"

"Stay out of trouble," she said.

I closed my eyes and automatically touched the inside of my lip with my tongue.

"Oh, sure. I will. Bye."

"You're welcome, Nathan."

"Thanks, mom. Bye."

"Nine o'clock. Bye."

I hung up.

Mel was already pulling black Creepers on his feet. "Okay! So what are we doing?"

"I'm really, seriously hungry," I said.

"Got any money?"

"Uh…" Last night had tapped me out.

Mel reached into his back pocket and flipped out his Rainbow wallet with a dramatic sigh. "I suppose I can cover us for Anarchy Burger."

I stood up and took Lina's hand. "I'll pay you back."

"Yeah, yeah, yeah…"

EIGHTEEN

We called it Anarchy Burger because of the twenty foot red "A" on the roof. Lina, Mel, and I placed our orders at the counter, then took a booth in the rear. I sat with my back to the wall and fiddled with the little plastic number they gave us to identify our order. Lina sat next to me, Mel across the table.

The smell of broiling cow flesh gave me a real salivation problem. I swallowed repeatedly.

Mel said, "So, what now? What are you going to do about Teslowski?"

I sighed. "Assuming he's not, like, in the hospital or something, I'm gonna have to talk to him."

Lina raised an eyebrow. "If he's as… capable as you think, he's probably not in the hospital." She smiled at me. "He's probably just moping over his wounds, same as you."

I grunted.

"Besides," she continued, "why bother talking to him? Didn't he set you up?"

I shook my head. "The more I think about it, I don't think he was there to fight me. I don't think he knew Felder and the others were gonna show up."

"How can you be sure?"

Mel laid a finger against the side of his nose like a New Romantic Santa. "The nose knows," he said.

"Right," I confirmed.

Lina shrugged. "He didn't have to fight you."

I frowned and looked at my hands. "Like Teslowski would back out of a fight. I practically forced him."

Lina put her chin in her hands. "How long has he had it in for you, anyway?"

Mel said, "They've been enemies almost as long as Nate and I have been friends."

"Has he ever tried to be friends with you before?"

I laughed. "I don't think he's looking to be friends—it was more like he wanted to compare notes. That, and he was… scared, I guess."

"Well, he's probably a little weirded out," Lina said. "Aren't you?"

The server brought our food then, and relieved me of the little plastic number. I willingly surrendered it in favor of my triple cheeseburger, which I set to instead of answering. I was too hungry for my throbbing lip to slow me down.

Mel bit open a ketchup packet and said, "I don't see why either one of you would be freaked out." He looked at Lina. "Imagine the two of them teamed up, running around Abbeque Valley like a couple of mystery men, or government spooks…"

I spoke with my mouth full. "What did you say?"

"Huh?"

"That word—'spooks.' What's that mean, anyway?"

"Oh, like, Roger Moore, or Maxwell Smart." Mel spoke through his nose: "Missed me by that much, Chief." He popped a French fry in his mouth. "You'd be Maxwell Smart, my friend. It's the hair."

"I just remembered Denver Colorado used that word to describe my dad."

Mel cocked his head and frowned. "Uh, non sequitur, Nate. Tallahassee Florida used the clock to climb the swimming pool."

Lina laughed and bumped her shoulder against mine. I told them both about meeting Denver at the cabin in Kirby Lake. "He called my dad 'that old spook.' I didn't think anything about it, then."

"Wild," said Lina. "You think your dad was some kind of CIA agent?"

"I don't know..." I shoved the rest of my burger into my mouth and wolfed it down while I thought. "My mother never said anything about it. Just that he died in a work accident."

Mel said, "Maybe she's been sworn to secrecy if she wants to keep the unmarked Swiss bank account?"

I allowed him a quick grin and slid out of the booth. "Lina, can we go back to my house? I want to ask her."

NINETEEN

It was just after eight when we walked through the door of my house. My mother was at the dining room table, working out of her briefcase.

"You're home early," she said. She looked up, saw my friends. "Hello, Mel… Lina, nice to see you again.

Lina held out her hand and my mother took it, which was strange to see. Parts of me were still in shock that I had a girlfriend.

My mother finally saw me. She paled, and rushed out of her chair.

"What the hell happened to you? I told you to stay out of trouble!" Automatically, she shot an accusatory glare at Mel, who held up his hands and stepped back.

"I'm fine, mom." I looked away from her stern inspection. "I… I got into a fight."

Her eyes widened and her sweat changed, tinged with alarm. "Is everyone all right?

"Everyone..?" That threw me off. "Yeah, I guess so. It was a draw, pretty much."

Her shoulders slumped and she expelled a short breath. "You're much stronger than kids your age, Nathan. You can't go around getting into fights. You know this."

"I didn't plan on it!"

She looked at the three of us. "This had already happened when you called me, hadn't it?"

I looked at my shoes. "Well, yeah."

She shook her head. "I knew we shouldn't have come back so fast. My own fault for listening to Denver."

That was an opportunity to shift the attention away from my fight with Teslowski, and I took it. "Actually, I wanted to, like, ask you about Denver."

"What do you want to know about him?" Her left eyebrow shot up.

Mel couldn't pass it up; he never could. "What's the annual snowfall there, anyway?"

My mother was used to ignoring him. Lina froze the involuntary smile on her face. She hadn't known Mel long enough, but she was learning.

I said, "Well, there was something he said when we were up there."

My mother was impatient. "What? What did he say to you?"

The whole vibe was making me very nervous. I swallowed.

"Did my dad work for the government, or something?"

"What? No."

Her answer was automatic. So was the change in her scent.

I looked at Lina. She took my hand.

"Mom. Why are you lying?"

Her eyes widened. "You'd better think about what you just said, Nathan."

I blanched. Her tone demanded that I back down, but the messages in her scent supported me.

It had been a weekend of new things. I was a bona-fide freak with a new name for what I was. I had a gorgeous older girlfriend. Why stop short of defying my mother?

"I—I know you're not telling the truth, mom. I can tell. You told me he was an independent contractor. For the government?"

Her eyes flashed. "Among other clients," she snapped. "I won't have you calling me a liar, Nathan. I don't care if your friends are here or not."

Lina squeezed my hand and let go. I kept my eyes on my mother. "That Denver guy called my dad 'that old spook.' Doesn't that mean 'spy?'"

"Denver Colorado. " She snarled the name. "You don't know him."

I looked at Lina and Mel. Mel bunched his shoulders and looked like he'd rather be anywhere else. Lina hugged herself and met my eyes, unwavering.

"I think you're leaving something out, mom."

My mother's eyes narrowed. She looked at Lina and Mel.

"You two should leave. Now. This is a family matter."

Mel went directly to the door. Lina nodded at me and followed him out.

My mother sat down at the table and made her paperwork into a neat stack. "Now it's just you and me." She put the stack into her briefcase and closed it. "Now we can talk."

I sat across the table from her. "Good."

She pointed at my bruised face. "Tell me what happened here."

"I thought we were going to…"

"This first."

I sighed.

"There's this kid. Byron Teslowski. He's been on my case for, like, forever. When I was out with Lina last night, he showed up at Belltower Plaza and said he wanted to meet. I said yes."

"You made a date to fight." My mother crossed her arms over her chest.

"No..! He said he only wanted to talk, and we did. He told me… he said he thought he might be a Sovereign, and since I probably was, he wanted to, like, talk about that and stuff."

"What makes this kid think he's a Sovereign? And what makes him think you are?"

I looked at her. "Mom. C'mon."

Her mouth turned down. "We'll leave that. What makes him think he's a Sovereign?"

"We didn't have time to get into that. He's got these friends. We call them his Wingmen, 'cause they're always hanging around with him, getting into stuff. They saw his car on the street and came up into the park. They kinda egged him on."

"Peer pressure."

"I guess; whatever. Thing is, when we started to fight, he was just like anyone." I tensed up just thinking about it. "I mean, I was way faster, stronger, all that. But as it went on… he got better."

She leaned forward in her chair, elbows on the table. "What do you mean, 'he got better?'"

"I mean, he ended up just as fast as me, and just as strong." I touched my lip. "Better, maybe. I really think he's like me… it was too weird."

My mother looked away for a second. I saw a million thoughts pass over her face. She looked back at me. "You can't go around getting into fights, Nathan."

"I wasn't!" I knew I sounded like a little kid.

She rubbed her temples. "You should have walked away."

I clicked my tongue and threw up my arms. "Why? I am always walking away, mom. Always." I shook my head. "I've let Teslowski and Felder and all the rest of those jerks say whatever they want, do whatever they want—I'm always turning the other, whatever, the other cheek, just because I'm not supposed to act like I'm any different."

"It's the best way," she said. She reached across the table to touch my hand.

I stood up before she could get to me. "Why? Since when is it okay to run away and let assholes get away with shit?"

Even through my anger, I instantly regretted using profanity with her. She must have known I was seriously upset, because she let it go. "Because you have a responsibility. You're better than everyone else in so many ways—you're stronger, faster, you know that—but you're smarter than most, too, Nate. Smart enough to rise above."

I choked on bitter laughter. "Oh, sure. I'm so far above it no one ever even talks to me, aside from a few people."

My mother's expression softened. "A few people like Lina?"

This disarmed me. I blushed automatically.

"Do you know what she said to me, first thing?"

"I don't."

"She said I had beautiful eyes."

"She's a smart girl."

Thinking about Lina drained the anger out of me. I knew there was a good chance my mother had done this deliberately, but I didn't mind all that much.

"Last night… you know how my eyes, like, catch the light, and stuff?"

"Right."

"She loves that." I sat back down. "She likes how I'm different, mom. Why should I bother to act like I'm not? Why can't I just be who I am?"

"It's not that simple."

There was so much going on in her head she wasn't saying. I didn't understand it.

"So, about my father..?"

She rubbed her forehead and pinched the bridge of her nose. "I've told you that your father was a scientist, a researcher. He worked for the Department of Defense. He was a consultant on a number of projects."

"So why would Denver call him a spook? A spy?"

"Your father couldn't talk about the work he did. A lot of it was classified." She stared off into elsewhere. "He would spend weeks out at Rachel, in the desert, and I had no idea what he was doing."

"You said he had an accident."

Her eyes regained their focus. She looked at me, folded her hands on the table, and sighed. "There was some kind of industrial accident. He was… burned."

She was still avoiding something, but I couldn't tell if it was just because the memory was painful. I didn't need my crazy senses to know she hated talking about it.

"You never told me that part."

She nodded, looked at her hands. "He never even got to see you."

"Yeah."

I squirmed a little in my seat. "Did he know about the… the stuff when I was born?"

"Oh, of course." She smiled. "It's not unheard of for an infant to be born with a little tail, or hair on its body."

"It's pretty rare to have both, though, isn't it?"

"Well…"

"Yeah."

I let her take my hands this time.

"Nathan, your father loved you. He was counting the days until he could come back home. He didn't care about your little… accessories. He thought you were perfect." Her mouth went shaky and she looked away. "You were just what he'd hoped for."

I felt bad, making her remember it all. I put on a smile. "Thanks. I really don't know why I've been thinking about it." I knew I still didn't have all the answers, but I was coming away from our talk with more than I'd had. "It's just—with this whole Sovereign thing, and Teslowski, and Lina, all at once—it's been crazy."

She smiled. "I know."

I yawned, slow and long.

"You've got school tomorrow," my mother reminded me. "It's going to be a big day."

I hadn't been to school since Thursday. Declaration Day.

"Yeah. I know."

"You don't have to go, if you don't want to."

I wondered how many kids had mothers hoping they'd ditch class. I laughed, stood up, and stretched. "No way, mom." I kissed the top of her head. "I'm totally ready to deal with whatever."

I suddenly realized this had been a really cool long weekend.

"And everybody's gonna have to deal with me, too."

TWENTY

Monday would be my first day back to school since the Donner Declaration. I woke up before my alarm went off, fueled up with my usual giant breakfast, and was the first kid to the bus stop. School's not the friendliest place for me, but that day, I was looking forward to being there.

The other kids at the bus stop didn't say anything to me, but that was nothing new… most of them were freshmen, for one thing, and let's face it, I'm me—no one really goes out of their way to say "hey."

Getting on the bus, though, thing were definitely out of the ordinary. The other kids watched me, whispering, which was the norm, but the mocking giggles were missing. Eyes were on me, but there was no derision, no cold stares. They were confused, and maybe curious. Definitely freaked out.

I didn't need my superhuman senses to know that I disturbed them.

I liked it.

I made my way to the last seat on the bus, the long bench where Mel and Jason waited. Jason hadn't seen me since Claire's get together last Thursday, when I met Lina, and a lot had happened since then.

Mel must have filled him in. He held his hand up for me to shake and said, "Dude," with a little nod and smile.

I clasped hands with him and sat down. "How's it going?"

Jason snorted. "You tell me, kicking Byron Teslowski's ass!"

I touched my lip, which was already almost healed. "It was more like a tie," I said, and looked at Mel.

He shrugged. "He didn't cut you with his bare hands, is all I'm saying."

Jason laughed, and shook his head. "That's too cool."

I nudged Mel with my shoulder. "What did you tell him?"

"That you and Teslowski got into it, and he left before you did."

"And that you tore him up with your fuckin' fingernails, dude!"

I sighed. Somehow, my friends celebrating all of this made me uncomfortable, even if I dug the fact that the rest of the kids on the bus seemed mellow. I was confused.

"He got his licks in," I mumbled.

Fortunately, Jason had the attention span of a dog. "Oh, hey, dude, what's up with you and that Lina chick?"

Again, I looked at Mel. He shrugged and held up his hands. "What? We're sitting here, Jason asks me what's up, I'm gonna tell him!"

"So, are you guys, like, going together, or what?"

My involuntary Lina smile slipped onto my lips. "Yeah, I guess."

Jason punched me in the shoulder. "Sweet!"

"Yep."

Jason looked thoughtful, but his eyes were full of mirth. "Of course, if you hadn't been there that day…"

Mel laughed. "If Nate hadn't been there, you would have had your face slapped, minimum."

Jason took it with a sideways nod. "No, I'm totally stoked for you, dude. Pretty big weekend, huh?"

"No question," I said.

The bus pulled into the school parking lot. Mel nudged me and pointed out the window.

"Look who's here."

Terrance Felder stood on the curb. He watched kids as they got off the bus. His fists were clenched and a big purple vein bulged on his bull neck.

My stomach quivered automatically. I swallowed and remembered what I was, what I could do, and what I'd learned over the last few days. I thought about Lina, and the pale look on Byron Teslowski's face when I cut him.

Jason said, "Dude, he's totally waiting to call you out."

I shrugged and shouldered my backpack. We got off the bus.

Felder barreled up to me. "Charters! You're dead meat, freak!"

He reached out with a flat hand to push me. He was slow. I grabbed him by the wrist and held on.

His face scrunched with confusion. "What're you doing, faggot?"

I tightened my grip, just a little. His arm was cold and soft, covered with freckles. I never knew he was more fat than muscle. It made me cocky.

"How's Byron, Terrance?"

His face went red. "Fuck you, asshole." He swiped with his free hand. I ducked and twisted his arm behind his back, then gave him a push. He stumbled forward a few feet.

A crowd gathered. They formed a tight ring around us.

"... check out freako..."

"... thinks he's all bad ass..."

"... Felder'll mess him up..."

"... fuckin' thinks he's Bruce Lee, or whatever..."

Felder twisted around. "I'm gonna kick your ass, Charters."

Over his shoulder, I saw the discipline advisor, Ms. Elp, striding toward us as fast as her Tartan skirt would allow. "Not today," I said.

Felder rushed me. All I had to do was step aside; momentum took care of the rest. He fell right into the ring of kids. They pushed him back.

People laughed, and they weren't laughing at me.

Someone said, "Lay off, Terry."

It was Byron Teslowski. The crowd let him through.

Our eyes met. He nodded.

"Byron, dude," Felder whined, "what's the deal?"

The circle of kids recoiled from Ms. Elp like they were afraid to touch her. "The deal," she said, "is that you two are done." She pointed a long finger at the spot between my eyes. "In my office, Nathan. I want to talk to you."

To me?

"But I…"

"In my office." She turned her back and started toward the school. "You too, Terrance." She didn't break her stride. She knew we would follow.

TWENTY-ONE

I was first in. I'd been in Ms. Elp's office before, but I was never the one who was in trouble. The framed prints of Scotland on the walls always reminded me of a travel agent's office.

With a sharp glance, she indicated a chair, and I sat down.

"I wasn't..."

"My office," she interrupted. She sat down behind her desk. "I get to go first."

My adrenaline still flowed. The muscles of my thighs jumped. I took a breath.

She steepled her hands and smiled without showing her teeth. "You missed some school last week. Pretty big day around here."

I knew what she meant. "Everywhere, I guess."

She nodded. "What do you think about all of that?"

"About... about William Donner?"

"Right."

I shrugged. "I dunno... it's pretty hard to believe?" This wasn't what I expected.

"Really?" I didn't understand the glint in her eye.

"I guess, yeah. I mean, if he can really do all that stuff, it's pretty... unbelievable, I guess."

"Oh, I don't know." One eyebrow shot above the frames of her glasses. "It seems to me it's best we keep an open mind, don't you think?"

I'm not stupid, and I knew she didn't think I was. We were playing some kind of game. After the thing with Terrance, I wasn't in the mood.

"Am I in trouble, Ms. Elp? Because, I didn't start that fight."

"I'm trying to figure out if you are in trouble, Nathan." She sat back and crossed her arms. "We've always made certain allowances for you, and your condition."

"My condition?"

"You know what I mean, Nathan. The school has accommodated you as best as we can."

"Accommodated me?" I didn't usually get upset with my teachers, or staff like Ms. Elp or the principal, but my blood was still hot… maybe since Sunday, even. "How?"

She looked at me for a moment, a slight warning in her eyes, before she spoke.

"You've always dealt with the other kids very well. Handled yourself with restraint." She leaned forward. "Dignity, I would even say."

"Being responsible," I said, a little curl in my lip. I looked at the floor.

"Yes." She slapped the desk with her palms and sat up. "Exactly. I've admired your maturity… which is why I was so disappointed when I saw it was you in the middle of that little scuffle out there."

"Felder was waiting for me!"

"Did you have to meet him?"

"I had to get off the bus..!"

She nodded once. "I'll grant you that—but you could have kept walking. You could have ignored him. You could have acted the way you've acted since your first day at this school." She picked up a pen and tapped it against her hand. "What's different now, I wonder?"

I finally got where she was going with this whole talk, and I could tell she knew I'd figured it out. I didn't like her manipulating the whole conversation. I didn't want to say what she wanted me to say, which was basically unfair, since it was exactly how I felt. It was a stupid game.

She said, "I'm expecting an answer."

"Yeah."

She clicked the pen open and arranged some papers on her desk. "We can sit here all day, if you like. I've got things I can do."

I huffed.

"You want me to say I think I can act differently now, now that these… Sovereign, or whatever, are out there. You think I think I don't have to take all the… the crap people give me, 'cause Donner, or whatever, will, like, look after me. Right?"

"Is that what you think?"

"No! But…" I spread my arms and let them drop. "You don't know how sick I am, letting everybody walk all over me, talk about me, make fun of me, just because I look the way I look!"

Maybe I was coming down from the thing with Felder, maybe it was being in Elp's office, maybe it was the whole thing, the last few days catching up. I have no idea why, really, but I actually started to cry. Once I realized it was happening, I was so mortified, it just made it worse.

"Half those jerks—hell, most of 'em—they don't have, like, any idea what I can do, who I am, what I am. I can hear every word they say to each other! Every word!" I sniffed and ran a quick hand under my nose. "I can tell people like Terrance Felder and Byron Teslowski are coming just by the way they smell, I'm so used to their crap!

"They think I'm just some skinny, freaky kid who stays away from everybody else, but I know I'm stronger than them, faster, smarter…"

"Better?"

She made me jump. I felt tight, bound up inside.

"Yeah, damn it!"

Ms. Elp looked at me. She stared at me for so long, her face totally unreadable, her scent masked by the awful perfume she wore, that I finally sat back in my chair and looked away. We stayed that way for a while.

"Nathan."

"What?" I wiped my face on my arm.

"The only talent you could possibly have that would matter at all in your life—the only real difference you should recognize between you and those kids who bother you—is humility."

"What?"

"It must be pretty frustrating for you, always turning the other cheek while this man in Washington makes fools of so many people in a single afternoon."

"I… guess." I'd never thought of it that way, and I wasn't sure I agreed, but I had to say something.

"You know, I saw in the paper that President Reagan is meeting with this Donner person. Do you know what this says to me?"

I shrugged.

"It says to me that Donner got the respect he wanted by being tough. By scaring us. He's a bully, just like that boy who was waiting for you this morning."

I knew she was getting to some point. I waited.

"The difference between him and you, Nathan, is that he seems to have some kind of supernatural powers. He can back up his talk."

I shrugged again. "Okay."

"I'll tell you what I think you have in common, though. I would bet that William Donner is a very lonely man. He wants people to respect him, and his people, and he's using his power to get what he thinks is respect from the whole world.

"He's probably talking to the President even as we speak. But I'm betting that the President doesn't really respect him. I'm betting President Reagan is afraid of him, even though he's the leader of the free world. He's being bullied. That's not respect; that's not really what Donner wants."

"So?"

She frowned. "Do I really have to spell it out for you, Nathan? You're brighter than that."

I didn't say anything.

She pursed her lips. "The point is that people respect those who handle themselves respectfully. Not grandstanding. Not bullying. By knowing their own strength, and standing on that. Not pushing it on others."

I nodded. I agreed with her, but I was still mad. "Are you going to give this same speech to Terrance Felder? He might know a little bit about being a bully, y'know?"

She narrowed her eyes. I was pretty well conditioned to respond to authority figures. I shrank a little in my chair.

"Here's the bottom line, Mister Charters. I want you to know that I will not tolerate anything like the showing off I saw from you this morning. You want to act like that, you want to show everyone how much stronger and faster you are, I'll be right there with the detentions, and parent conferences, and suspensions, and eventually I'll see you expelled. I will not have you disrupting this school. Learn to deal with yourself, be an adult, or get out of this school. Do you understand me?"

I nodded again. I knew she was right, but it seemed pretty damn unfair to me. If I was really a Sovereign, was that good for anything, or not?

The first period bell rang. Ms. Elp wasn't quite done.

"You know more than you did before last Thursday. There's no excuse."

She scrawled on a hall pass and handed it over to me. "Get to class. I don't want to have this discussion with you again."

I took the hall pass and stood up.

"Thanks."

She tilted her head to the door. "Tell Terrance to come in here on your way out."

Felder stood up when he saw me come out. He glared at me and balled up his fists. I glared right back at him, but I hoped he couldn't tell I'd been crying.

"Don't fuck with me again, Felder." I was just loud enough for him to hear.

His eyes widened.

I liked that. I wanted to shock him. I wanted to shock everyone. I hoped word of our fight would spread around the whole school. If it did, maybe I wouldn't have to do anything that would land me back in Ms. Elp's office.

TWENTY-TWO

Every teacher worked the Donner Declaration into the lesson that day. My third period Civics teacher, Mr. Pfalger, actually made us watch a video of the whole deal, like we hadn't seen it fifty million times already.

When it was over and Pfalger switched the lights back on, my pupils contracted to slivers. I blinked until they adjusted to almost normal, their slightly oval shape almost unnoticeable. It was an automatic thing to not want people to notice another thing different about me, and as soon as I did it, I wished I'd just let it go. It was time for people to get used to it.

Pfalger leaned against the edge of his desk and crossed his arms. We knew it was his lecture pose, so we put down our pens.

"So." He had a small smile on his lips. "What's everybody think? Is it the story of the century? Is it the end of the world? Is it just a big hoax?" He looked around the room. "Mister Helfinger—what's going on with this?"

Vinnie Helfinger shrugged. "I dunno."

Pfalger grinned. "That's obvious from your grades, Mister Helfinger, but take a stab anyway. What does the Donner Declaration make you think about? How does it make you feel?"

Vinnie looked like he was thinking about it. His considerable brow furrowed. "I guess… I guess it's pretty cool."

"Why?"

"Well, like, this Donner dude can do whatever he wants, right? That's pretty cool."

"Okay, sure. But technically, that's what Donner himself makes you feel. What about this declaration of his?"

The class was quiet. There was an uneasy tightness in my stomach. I felt a little like when people talk about you in the third person and you're standing right there.

Sandra Banuelos spoke up. "He… he thinks he's above the law."

Pfalger pointed at her with both hands and bounced into a pace. "That's an interesting phrase, 'above the law.' It implies some superiority, doesn't it? But that's not really what Donner said, is it? Remember, he declared that he… and everyone like him, and that's a whole other issue… is sovereign. What does that mean? What is a sovereign?"

This kid named Ken something or other put up his hand and said, "It's like the king, right? Like sovereign ruler."

"Not bad… close." Pfalger stopped pacing and clasped his hands together. "In the sixteenth and seventeenth centuries, the countries of Europe were trying to figure out how to deal with a secular, instead of religious, justification for their authority. Before then, you were king because God said you were, or in some cases, you were related to God, or maybe even a god yourself." He smiled. "Not unlike my own vast authority here in this classroom, right?"

I laughed along with a few others. Pfalger was tough on all of us, but he was fun.

"So it was determined, essentially—and I'm skipping a whole lot, here, since this isn't really the point of today's class—that every country was equal in stature to every other. That a country had a right to govern its own affairs." He paused and started pacing again, back and forth in front of his desk.

"Name a sovereign nation today."

Most folks said the United States, including me. Jeff Ford said, "All of 'em, right?"

Pfalger stopped dead. “All of them? Really? Even, say, Taiwan? Tibet? Romania? Yugoslavia? Are those countries equal in stature to other nations? Are they equal to, for example, China and the Soviet Union? For that matter, do they have a right to govern their own affairs?”

An uneven chorus of “no” carried across the room.

“Not so much, eh? So you can see, it’s more of an ideal than a reality. What makes one nation, say, more equal than others?”

Vinnie Helfinger had this one. “Power.”

Pfalger’s eyebrows went up and he smiled at Vinnie. “Nice one, Mister Helfinger. But it’s obvious, right? It’s the same on every level. China keeps Tibet under its thumb because China is much, much more powerful. We haven’t been invaded by Mexico, recently, because we’re much, much more powerful. Right?”

He didn’t wait for our response. “So what happens when a person speaks up and says that he’s a sovereign power all on his own—and he seems to be much, much more powerful than any other single person?”

We thought about it. Nobody knew. I sure didn’t know. I said as much.

Pfalger pointed at me. “That’s the whole drama right now, isn’t it? That’s why it’s such a big deal. Not because the ubermensch is alive and well and capable of damn near anything—it’s because the balance of power has been threatened, pretty brazenly, by one guy… and he’s still out there! He hasn’t been thrown in prison, or shot in the street, or disappeared… and why not?”

Sandra said, “We don’t do that to people.”

Pfalger shrugged. “Don’t we? Donner’s made some claims, hasn’t he, about what this country has already done to other people like him—it’s the whole reason he made his declaration, right?”

Sandra wasn’t convinced. “But maybe he’s just saying that.”

Pfalger shrugged, smiled. “Maybe. Put yourself in the government’s shoes. Let’s say you find out that some members of the population have powers, abilities, whatever they’re calling them, that give them an advantage over the norm. How would it make you feel?”

I thought about my mother's assumptions about the government. "Nervous," I said.

"Sure! Nervous… or, to put it another way: insecure." He emphasized the word with a fist into his open palm. "It would be a matter of national security, wouldn't it? Because order has to be maintained, right?"

He had us all thinking.

"So let's say, for sake of argument, that Donner's correct, and the government has known about these so-called Sovereign people for a while now, and yet for some reason their existence isn't common knowledge. Now that this guy who is apparently the most powerful of all these people comes forward and says, essentially, "don't tread on me," right? What happens now?"

"Isn't Donner meeting with the President today?" I said.

"Yep. Cool to be a fly on that wall, eh?" Some chuckles in the class. "I want you to really think this through: why would Reagan, who supposedly already knows about the Sovereign people and is maybe, just maybe keeping them under control somehow… why would he bother to meet with this self-proclaimed leader who essentially threatened the whole country on the President's front lawn?"

We all gave it some thought. I wasn't sure, myself. Up to then, I'd been thinking about what the whole thing meant to me, how it meant that I wasn't so much of a freak anymore… or at least, I was part of a group of freaks, which was a little better. But what did it mean in a bigger sense?

Pfalger said, "What happens when all these little Donners suddenly feel like it's okay to come out of the woodwork? What's it mean if the government can't get away with keeping this whole thing secret anymore? What if tomorrow it's not just Donner and this mysterious flying guy in New York—what if tomorrow it's your neighbor?"

I wanted to slouch in my chair, just a little. I looked around at my classmates. Some looked thoughtful. Some looked flat-out worried.

A few glanced at me, then looked away.

"Intriguing, isn't it?" Pfalger clapped his hands. "It's also your homework assignment. I want a five hundred word essay on what the Donner Declaration means to you and your place in the world." He looked right at me for a moment, just long enough to convey that his expectations were somehow different, or higher, with me. I tried to keep my expression blank.

"Think about it carefully. Due Wednesday. That's it."

The bell rang.

TWENTY-THREE

After spending so much quality time in her company that morning, I didn't really feel like eating lunch in my usual spot beneath Ms. Elp's office window. I found a low wall near the main entrance of the school, far from the nearest kids, and settled into my sack lunch.

Nobody came near me, no one noticed me… it felt like the first moment of peace I'd had the whole day. There was just too much attention on the whole Sovereign thing. Nobody came flat out and called me one, even though Elp and Pfalger came pretty close. Still, I could feel the difference in the way people looked at me. There wasn't simple mockery, or derision. Pitiful as it sounds, I was used to that, and I could ignore it. This was different. Curiosity. Fear, maybe even.

I thought I was ready to announce myself to the world, and to hell with anyone who had a problem with it. Even without my own little declaration, it was turning into a really long day.

I was almost through with lunch when I caught Teslowski's scent. He came around the corner, following the light breeze, a moment later.

We looked at each other. It was a little weird to realize I didn't feel any anxiety about him any more. I put down my food and inclined my head.

"Hey."

"Hey." He swung a leg over the wall and sat down, facing me. "Sorry about Terry."

I shrugged. "It's cool. You… all right, or whatever?"

He touched his stomach. "Yeah. I heal up real fast."

"Oh." That figured. I did, too. I wondered if it was a Sovereign thing.

We looked around. I didn't know what to say. It was awkward. Finally Teslowski said, "Listen, Charters, those guys aren't gonna hassle you anymore, okay? Me neither."

I felt such a strong, automatic rush of relief, it was embarrassing. Six years of shit from this guy was over? It was too good to be true.

"I'm… uh, glad to hear that." It was an understatement. I found myself smiling.

He laughed. He seemed a little embarrassed himself. "Yeah, well, it was fucked up. Our fight, too."

"Yeah. Sorry about that."

"No biggie."

More weird silence. I scratched my head. "Look, Teslowski, I don't really know what else to say. Are we supposed to be friends again?"

He squinted and looked across the parking lot. "Things are gonna get weird, maybe. Don't you think?"

I was beginning to. "Maybe."

He nodded. "You and me, we should watch each other's backs."

I watched him stare off into the middle distance. "You mean like allies?" That wasn't as big a stretch as friends.

"Yeah." He turned and looked at me. "Yeah, like allies."

He held out his hand. I shook hands with Byron Teslowski, a big moment of détente in the history of Abbeque Valley High, or at least in the life of Nathan Andrew Charters. I imagined Reagan and Donner, three thousand miles away in Washington, doing pretty much the same thing. I shook my head.

"This seem weird to you?"

He barked a short laugh. "Fuck, dude, it's a trip." His face clouded. "I mean it, though. We're cool?"

"Yeah, man, I guess we're cool." I cocked a thumb toward the school behind me. "What about your Wingmen?"

"Huh?"

That was funny. He didn't know about the nickname we'd given his little band of followers. "Felder, and the rest."

He shrugged. "Fuck 'em. They'll do as I say or they can fuck off."

"Aren't they your friends?"

"If they thought I was one of them Sovereign, they'd shit, dude."

That took me aback. "They don't know? What about your parents?"

He shook his head and looked me in the eye. "Just you, dude."

I realized it made sense. He could hide his differences behind natural talent… which I guess it was, after all. He didn't have to worry about big eyes that glowed in the dark, or hair that never grew. It was a pretty safe bet he didn't have a note in the nurse's office to excuse his funky metabolism.

He was pretty lucky.

"Who's gonna know, anyway, right?" I shrugged. "I don't know why you're worried. Nobody can tell you're any different."

The bell rang. Lunch was over. He stood up.

"How long's that gonna last?"

TWENTY-FOUR

Abbeque Valley is a planned community in Orange County, in Southern California. Basically, that means there are four or five different floor plans for the houses, everything has a red tile roof, and most of the street names are a random combination of two Spanish words. It's pretty boring.

The billionaires who designed the town did one cool thing, though. Most of the neighborhoods are broken up by these long, narrow areas that were never developed—they're like woods. I don't know if they call these places something different at city hall, but everybody I know just calls them the Glen.

Tuesday afternoon after school, I finished most of my homework. I just had Pfalger's essay to work on.

I sat at the kitchen table and stared at a blank piece of college-ruled for fifteen minutes. Finally, I grabbed my jacket, a pen, and a notebook, and headed down to the Glen that cut between Mel's street and mine. There's a clearing in there, with these big California oaks on every side, and a big dead tree that makes a nice place to sit. It's far enough from the street I can almost ignore the sounds of cars and stuff, too. I can think there.

Birds flitted back and forth in the branches above and yammered at me. I think there's something about my scent that pisses them off more than other people. It's funny.

The loamy soil filled my nostrils with warmth and comfort. A few yards away, a mouse darted back and forth in the bushes. I sighed. It felt good to be around wild stuff, even if it was suburban planned-community wild stuff.

I opened my notebook. This is what I wrote.

What the Donner Declaration Means To Me

By

Nate Charters

The Donner Declaration is probably the most important thing that's happened in my lifetime. Now that people know there are Sovereigns, I think a lot of things will change.

One thing that will make the world a different place is when the Sovereign people start to really show up. We might need new laws to learn how to live in a world where there are people with amazing powers.

Right now, William Donner, the first Sovereign, and President Ronald Reagan are holding talks in Washington D.C. Maybe that's what they're talking about. Also, if there are really powerful Sovereign people, our government might want some of them for the army, or the CIA. If they're like Donner, then our government would want them on our side. Maybe we want to make a Sovereign army before the Russians do.

I don't know if William Donner will want this to happen, though. His Declaration was more about people leaving the Sovereigns alone.

I stopped. This wasn't what the Donner Declaration meant to me. Not really. But how could I write about that, and not make a big announcement saying I thought I was a Sovereign, too? And if I did that, wouldn't I have to act like a Sovereign?

I didn't even know what that meant, really. Pfalger explained the definition of Sovereign, kind of, but what would it mean to really be one?

Ms. Elp thought William Donner was lonely. That made sense, in a way. If you were a whole nation, all by yourself, that would be pretty lonely. I wondered if he even thought of himself as an American.

Or a human.

Would I have to stop being an American? Would I have to be different than everyone else?

I already was. I had been my whole life. But how would it be to actually accept that? Embrace it?

I thought about how it felt when Byron Teslowski's skin broke and his warm blood slipped onto my fingers. I remembered the look on Terrance Felder's face when I grabbed his arm.

I took a deep breath. A thousand separate scents washed across me… the whole world, right there on the wind. No one else in the whole world knew what that was like… at least no one who walked on two legs.

I couldn't deny I was different. Times like this, I liked it. But I didn't want to be alone. When I hung out with Mel, or Jason… when I was with Lina, I didn't feel any different from her. Why should being different mean being apart?

A little smile came to my lips. I started writing.

I know what it's like to be different from everyone else, like Donner and the flying man in New York City. I know what it's like to be able to do things no one else can do. I've always looked different from everybody else, so if it turns out that I'm a Sovereign, the only thing that will really change is I'll be part of a group, part of a minority that's bigger than just me.

All the same, I'm still a person. I have a normal mom, and normal friends, and I don't see any reason why I should act like I should be set apart from them or the rest of the world. I want to be part of the world—I want people to take me for who I am.

I think William Donner is asking for trouble with his threats and demonstrations. I don't want to be segregated, and I think it's wrong for Sovereign people to try to segregate themselves. I don't even know if I like the name "Sovereign." It makes it sound like those people are better than everyone else.

I might find out that I'm technically a Sovereign person, but I don't want that name. I don't have Sovereign friends, I have friends who are as normal or not normal or unique as everyone else. So I want to be counted with them.

I stopped to count words. Almost four hundred. I could probably add more, but there wasn't anything else I really wanted to say.

I'd never written anything like this before. I read it over again, and it made me nervous. I pretty much came out and said I was a Sovereign. Even though I was sure Ms. Elp and Mr. Pfalger thought I was anyway, and the rest of the school probably suspected, it gave me a little scary thrill to actually put it down in black and white.

I hoped Pfalger wouldn't make me read it in class.

The cool, early Spring wind shifted, and with it came a scent like I'd never experienced. It was sharp, pungent, and tart. It made me jump to my feet with a shiver of adrenaline. I rocked back and forth on the balls of my toes and my body tried to decide to run or not.

It was almost dark in the late afternoon shadows under the trees. My eyes adjusted, but lack of light washes out colors, and sometimes, details. I looked around, but I couldn't see anything that would have such an odor.

My senses were confused. The scent had too much going on—it was like wet fur, and human sweat, and garbage, and old meat. All of those things together were just… wrong.

The birds weren't making any noise. When did they stop?

I tilted my head, the rest of my body frozen in a flight-or-fight crouch. There was no sound in the clearing. Nothing moved, or every living thing had high-tailed it. I couldn't tell.

It was just me. And whatever owned that scent.

In the bushes, a dark patch of shadows moved, just a little. A really big patch of shadows.

Every hair on my head stood straight up. My skin crawled. My lips pulled back from my teeth, and I could taste the shadow's scent on my tongue.

I backed away, then turned and ran for the street. I needed to get away from that thing, and out of the Glen.

I hit the sidewalk, out into the open air, and ran across the street. I gave myself another fifty feet or so before I stopped and turned around.

I couldn't see back into the clearing. From where I stood, the Glen looked like it always looked. I also couldn't catch the scent anymore.

I could still feel it, though, on the inside of my nostrils and in my throat. I shook my head, sneezed, and spat. Then I spat again, and again, and when my mouth was dry I bit the inside of my cheek to make more saliva. I spit that out, too.

I looked at the Glen. No change, except the birds sang again.

I took the long way home, on the sidewalk, and I kept the Glen on the opposite side of the street as much as I could. I didn't exactly run, but I walked pretty fast. When I got to my house, the driveway was empty, which I was grateful for. I wasn't ready to share.

I turned on the television just have some noise in the house. I found myself standing in the kitchen, at a loss.

What was that?

Something big was in the Glen, not thirty feet away from me, and whatever it was, it sneaked up on me. That's really hard. Even though it had the wind on its side until the end, I should have heard it.

I keep calling it "it." That's because I know it wasn't human. Not exactly. It was too wild, too feral. But it was as big as a man, and I was pretty sure it stood on two legs.

That scent haunted me. I realized the reason it startled me so much. At first, I thought it was because it was unique, like nothing I'd ever experienced before, and that was a shock.

Thing is, it wasn't really unique. It was too many familiar things. Animal. Human. Not enough of each, and too much of each.

Like me.

I felt a hot tear slide down my cheek. I couldn't explain it. I just stood there in the kitchen. My breath rushed in and out of my lungs.

Whatever that was, it was like me, in a way. Like me if I hadn't had a bath in five years. Like me if I was a homeless guy. Who ate raw meat. And never cleaned up.

"Shit," I whispered with a long, trembling sigh. Another Sovereign in Abbeque Valley? First Teslowski, super-jock, and now this… this bear-guy?

Maybe it was seeking me out. Maybe it caught the scent of a smaller version of itself, and wanted to check me out. Or eat me.

It was dark outside. I strode through the house and turned on all the lights. I couldn't decide if I was scared, or just really sad.

When my mother came home she asked me if I owned stock in Edison and snapped off most of the lights. She had a bucket of Piccolo Pat's Chicken. We ate dinner in front of the television and watched the news, which, apart from coverage that the Coca-Cola company was changing its recipe, was mostly speculation on the closed talks between Reagan and Donner. When I was done eating I took a shower and went right to bed. I didn't say a word about the thing in the Glen.

TWENTY-FIVE

Wednesday afternoon, Lina picked me up after school. We went to Anarchy Burger for an early dinner.

"Get whatever you want," she said.

"You sure about that?"

"Yup. I got some money from my mom."

I was pretty hungry, as usual. I ordered a triple cheeseburger, large fries, a strawberry milkshake, onion rings, and a soda. Lina ordered a plain hamburger, small fries, and an iced tea, so she finished well before I did. I was about two thirds of the way through my meal when I noticed she was looking at me with a little smile on her face, her chin propped on one hand.

"When I said get whatever you want, I didn't mean get everything on the menu." She laughed.

"Told you about my metabolism," I said around a mouthful of cheeseburger.

"Dinner with you is a spectator sport, Nate."

I shrugged and smiled.

Once she saw I was pretty much finished, Lina said, "So did you get your essay back from Pfalger?"

"Yeah!" I pulled it out of my backpack and passed it across the table to her. "He gave me a C! Can you believe that? I practically come right out and say I'm a Sovereign, and he gives me a freakin' C!"

Lina granted me a sympathetic pout and looked at the essay. "He crossed out the whole first part."

"Yeah. When he handed it back to me, he's like, 'you would have got an A if you'd done the whole thing on topic.'"

Lina smiled. "You know what that means, right?"

I shrugged again.

"Pfalger got it," she said. "He used to teach over at O'Neil; I know what he's like. He couldn't give you a good grade since you didn't really follow the directions. Half of this thing is what the Donner Declaration means to the rest of the world, not to you." She handed the paper back to me. "You're lucky you didn't get an F. A C means he's on your side."

I gave the essay another look. "Huh." I smiled. "You think so?"

"Yeah, sure. Now everybody knows…"

That thought still gave me mixed feelings. "Yeah." I hadn't told Lina, or anyone, about the… whatever it was I'd encountered the day before. I'd been thinking more about it being some kind of homeless Sovereign, living like a bum because it was too different to fit in. I didn't want that to be me one day.

Lina looked at me. "What's up."

"I guess I really have to deal with it."

She nodded, looked down at her plate. She found a remaining French fry and twirled it in ketchup. She looked up at me through her bangs.

"Your mom's gonna be pissed."

TWENTY-SIX

Friday afternoon at school, I responded to a call on the public address system to report to the office. It was seventh period, my free period, and since there was no Open Door at Claire's, Mel and I hung around in the commons and kept our heads down.

"What's that about?"

I stood up and shouldered my backpack. "I don't know." I looked across the way to Ms. Elp's window, but the discipline advisor wasn't in her office. "I guess I'll see you later…"

"Yeah. Good luck!"

"Right."

I walked across the commons to the offices, confused. I had spent the entire week behaving myself. I avoided Byron Teslowski, which kept Terrance Felder and the rest of the Wingmen out of my hair. I underplayed my strength and agility even more than usual during P.E., and tried my best to stay alert and awake through all of my classes.

The week I "came out" to Abbeque Valley High, I tried my best to act as normal as anyone.

When I got to the reception area, I was doubly confused to see my mother. She smiled, so I relaxed a little, but there was tension in her face.

"Sorry, Nate. I'm taking you home today."

I shrugged. "I don't get to ride the bus? Darn!"

We walked outside and down the long steps to the parking lot. "Your friend wasn't giving you a ride today, was she?"

I shook my head. "Lina? No… she's got, like, some thing with her mother. So I don't mind you coming… but what's the occasion?"

"There's going to be a press conference in about forty five minutes," she said as we got into the car. "It's about William Donner. I wanted you to be able to see it, and you wouldn't get home in time if you waited for the bus."

"You don't think they'd just repeat it?"

She pulled out of the parking lot and flipped on AM radio. "I want you to hear it the first time," she said. "It's not every day history is made. You should experience it when it happens."

I gave a short laugh. "Seems like these days, it is every day."

She tilted her head. "Hm."

Like so often since the Donner Declaration, my mother and I sat in front of the television. Press Secretary Speakes stood in front of the cameras and announced what we would eventually call the Sovereign Compromise.

Essentially, the United States declared the Sovereign people would have political status similar to Native Americans. Even though Donner wanted them to be separate from the laws of the country, they worked it out that no Sovereign could ever be declared less than human or less than citizens.

The Sovereign nation, such as it was, would be led by Dr. William Karl Donner. No big surprise there. He would be the official arbitrator and representative when dealing with the government.

Meanwhile, Donner agreed to make any information he had about Sovereign people, including where they came from, abilities, and any new discoveries, available to the government, and they would do the same.

Finally, just like Donner had said in the Declaration, Sovereign people would be responsible for their actions. Donner would put together a kind of police force to handle Sovereign people who broke laws of the United States. This same police force would be available to help the government when Sovereign types threatened national security.

"Meet the new boss," my mother mumbled.

"Huh?"

"This is a pretty strange arrangement, Nathan, don't you think?" She shook her head at the television. "It's almost like Donner backed down…"

"But what…"

"Shh!"

A reporter had asked about the jurisdiction of this proposed Sovereign police force. Speakes replied they would solely be responsible for the actions of other Sovereign, and while they would work with local and national law enforcement agencies, they would answer to Dr. Donner and the Sovereign authorities.

My mother laughed and shook her head. "Who watches the watchmen? It's like the damn Justice Corps."

"You're losing me, mom."

She looked at me. "In the fifties, before the comic books were put out of business by the Wertham Act, there was one where all the mystery men banded together to fight the bad guys. They called themselves the Justice Corps. Your Uncle Greg read them, and then he'd pass them on to me. There was one story where they all decided that, since they had these amazing powers and were dedicated to fighting evil and righting wrongs, they might as well take control of the country."

I looked at the television and got a little chill. "What happened?"

"I don't know. The Wertham Act drove the comics publishers out of work. They never finished the story." She shrugged. "Until now."

"I don't know if the Sovereigns could take over the country."

"If Donner really is able to make whatever he thinks into reality, he could do it himself, Nathan."

"I don't know," I said. "I mean, if that's the case, why are we even cooperating with him? Why haven't we just stopped him somehow?"

She shook her head. "I don't know. I just know there has to be more going on here than we're being told. There always is."

I couldn't argue with that.

"So, what do you think it's gonna mean, like, for me?"

"For you?"

"Well, yeah. What's it mean to be a Sovereign?""

She looked at the television. "Who ever said you were a Sovereign person, hot shot?"

My mouth dropped open. "What? You're the one who got all freaked out when this whole thing started going down, all worried that the government would come and try to do something to me! Why would they if I wasn't a Sovereign?"

She smiled cleverly. "The longer you deny you're a Sovereign, the better chance you have of living a normal life. You don't want to live on a reservation somewhere, do you?"

"So, now I'm not a Sovereign?"

"Not as far as these bastards are concerned," she said. Her smile stiffened to a thin line. "It's all about keeping you off the radar."

I thought about school, about the looks I'd been getting and the comments I heard in the halls. I thought about my essay for Pfalger, and my talk with Ms. Elp.

"Um…"

The phone rang. My mother got up and answered it.

"Oh, hello, Ms. Elp," she said. I sat up straight and strained to hear both ends of the conversation. I could do that, sometimes, if there was no other noise in the house. With the television on, I really didn't stand a chance, and it would be a little conspicuous to turn it down.

"No, it's not that late—except for you; you're burning some late oil… yes, as a matter of fact we're watching it now." My mother had her polite phone voice on, but as she listened, her face hardened and her tone darkened. "Of course you will. Right. Of course." Her knuckles were white against the receiver.

"I appreciate your doing that, Camille. Right. Good bye."

She hung up and glared at me.

"What have you been telling them at school, Nathan?"

"Nothing." Shit.

"Really."

"Uh, yeah."

"Then why would Ms. Elp call to assure me the school would do everything they could minimize any disruption the Sovereign Compromise might cause you?" She took a step toward me, her arms rigid at her sides. I hadn't seen her mad like this for a really long time. "Why did she tell me that she'd work with me to make sure the school followed any regulations that came down in the coming weeks? Why did she go out of her way to call me at almost five thirty in the evening to tell me that Abbeque Valley High and the Abbeque Valley School District was committed to respecting your new status, whatever that would come to mean?"

I stood up. I didn't feel comfortable sitting down when she was like this. I mean, she had never hit me or anything, but I didn't like how small I felt.

"Mom…"

"Well?"

I spread my arms and shrugged. "I mean… look, she's just assuming the obvious, right? I mean, it's, like, obvious I'm not like other kids. She knows—all the teachers know—that I've got stuff I can do that's different from everybody else." I sighed, exasperated. "Heck, mom, all you have to do is look at me!"

She relaxed slightly. She couldn't argue with anything as obvious as the way I looked. "Well." She crossed her arms, turned her head, and her eyes lost focus as she thought. "Well." She looked at me. "Fine. But I don't want you to admit to being anything other than *Homo sapiens*. Don't let anyone label you as Sovereign."

I nodded. "I don't want anyone to treat me any different, mom. But between you and me, I probably am one of them, right? I mean, what other explanation is there?"

She sat down on the couch. I sat down next to her. We looked at the television, which had switched to world reaction to the Sovereign Compromise.

"We'll have to wait and see," she said with a sigh. "Nobody is forced to proclaim themselves one race or another in this country, so I can't see them forcing you to register yourself..." She shook her head and frowned. "God help us if it comes to that, though."

We'd studied the Holocaust in school. I knew what she was getting at. "They wouldn't do that."

She gave me a sympathetic look. It was the kind of look you give a little kid when he says something cute.

"Well, they wouldn't!"

"We'd better hope so." She slapped her knees and stood up. "I think it's time to get cracking on this stuff."

"What... what do you mean?"

"I'm not sure yet." She tapped the tip of her chin with an index finger. "Monday, though, I think I'm going to make some calls."

"To who?" She was making me just slightly nervous.

"The ACLU, for starters," she said. "I've got some friends. They can give me some idea of what's going on out there." She pointed at the television. "Over there."

"Oh."

The phone rang again. My mother answered it. "Hello? Yes, hold on." She pointed to me with the receiver. "It's Lina."

I shot off the couch and scooped the phone from my mother.

"Hey!"

"Hey yourself," she said. I could hear the smile in her voice, and it made me happy. "Are you busy tonight, boyfriend?"

That word still brought out a little involuntary chuckle out of me. "I don't think so. Why?"

"There's a party at my friend Car's house," she said. "I've been wanting you to meet him, and stuff. You wanna?"

"Well, sure!"

"Cool. You can call Mel and Jason, see if they want to, too. Those boys need to get out of the house."

I laughed. "Yeah, okay. Lemme check... hold on, okay?"

"I'm not going anywhere," she said.

I cupped the mouthpiece with one hand. "Mom. Is it alright if I go out with Lina tonight?"

"Tonight..?" She looked at the television. People were lighting cars on fire in some city somewhere.

I frowned. "Mom. It's here, you know?"

She frowned right back. "When were you expecting to be home?"

"Well, it's Friday night…"

"Just when, Nathan? Give me something."

"Um… one?"

She stared at me just long enough, I thought I'd made a ridiculous request. I was gearing up to give ground by an hour when she said, "One o'clock. And it's you and Lina? Where?"

"A party at her friend's house. Mel and Jason'll be there too."

"A drinking and drugs kind of place?"

"It's Lina's friend, mom."

She tilted her head and her eyebrows shot up. "And that means what?"

I sighed, acutely aware that I was keeping Lina waiting on the phone. "Okay, I don't know what kind of party it is. But you know I won't be doing anything, no matter what, right?"

"Hm." She nodded. "Yes, I do know that." Her lips twitched up at the corners. "One o'clock. I'm not waiting up. Don't be late."

"Cool!" I got back to Lina. "I can go… when?"

"I'll come get you in an hour and a half," she said. "I haven't gotten ready yet. I wanted to make sure you could come."

I smiled. "So, you wouldn't have gone if I couldn't?"

"We maybe could have done something else… but I'm glad you can go. I really want you to meet Car."

"You're a sweetie," I said. "I'll call Mel and Jason."

"See you soon, cutie," she said.

We hung up.

What was I supposed to wear to a party? What kind of party was it? And I still didn't know: who, exactly, was this Car guy, to Lina?

TWENTY-SEVEN

Sometimes, she stopped my heart. Lina wore a picnic-blanket summer dress of little red and white squares that came to just above her calves. Her black platform pumps made her a few inches taller than me. She was made up a little more than usual, powder pale with dark red lips. Her blonde hair was slicked back tight on her scalp.

I was with this woman!

She took my arm and we strode up to Carson Meunetti's house with Mel and Jason in tow. A deluge of rapid-fire punk rock and a dozen conversations, along with the thick, sweet smell of beer and cigarettes, escaped when the door opened. A tall, lanky guy with spiked, sandy blonde hair stepped out.

"Hey, Car!" Lina disengaged herself from me and gave him a hug.

"Hey, Lina." His smile was bright and wide on his narrow face. It faltered slightly when he saw me. I think my eyes were doing their reflective thing in the porch light. "You brought some friends?"

We stepped inside as Lina made introductions. She grabbed my arm and beamed, which made me feel nice.

"This is my very good friend Nathan, and his friends Jason and Mel."

Car shook my hand. He looked me in the eye and his smile was solid again. "Nice to meet you, Nathan."

I couldn't tell you why, but I liked this guy instantly. "Likewise, Carson. Call me Nate."

"Well, then, call me Car." He shook Mel and Jason's hands. "Gentlemen."

Mel said, "I caught your band at the Rail, a couple months back."

Car looked pleased. "Oh, cool. That's a fun place."

Jason scanned the crowd as he spoke. "What kind of stuff do you guys do?"

"Mine," Car said with a laugh. On the stereo, someone proclaimed they had the neutron bomb, over and over again. "Oops," our host said. "This one skips; I forgot. Excuse me. Have fun." He bounded for the turntable.

Lina led me into the kitchen, Mel and Jason on my heels. A couple near the refrigerator, all hairspray, leather, and androgyny, were too distracted with each other to do more than favor us with blank glances.

Lina didn't hesitate. "Scuze," she said, and slipped past them. She opened the fridge and pulled out two bottles of beer with a familiarity that made me think she knew this house very well. She handed me one.

"Oh." I stared at the yellow bottle.

Her smile was huge. "Let me corrupt you, Nate, just a little bit." She pulled a magnetic bottle opener off the side of the fridge and handed it to me. I used it, and handed it to Mel.

"I'm in your hands," I said to Lina.

She leaned in close and muttered in my ear, "Maybe later."

I put the bottle to my smiling lips. An hour later, I had the first buzz of my young life. I felt confidant, and special, if a little off-balance. I was with a beautiful girl who knew all these way-cool people, and she made a point of introducing me to everyone with a pride that was charmingly defiant.

I thought my crowd at school were misfits. In fact, we were all just geeks compared to this bunch with their black clothes, studded jewelry, painted Levis, multicolored hair, and tattoos. I had been a little intimidated, but the beer relaxed me, and anyway, no one seemed to care about my obvious differences. For a while.

Lina went to the bathroom. Over the heavy reverb thrashing sound of a guy I was told was Darby Crash, a scarecrow all in black nodded to me and asked, "Are you one of them?"

My hackles rose, but he wasn't really threatening. He smiled at me and swayed, and his eyes didn't quite keep pace with where he wanted to look.

I bared my incisors, which are just slightly longer and sharper than yours. "What do you think?"

"Fuck me," he breathed. "What do you do?"

I decided to turn dumb, since it was a pretty direct question from a stranger. When Teslowski asked me, it had been different—we had a long history, even if it was a history of abuse and torment.

"I go to Abbeque Valley," I said innocently.

He laughed. I could smell vomit on his breath. "No, dude… I mean, what can you do?"

"Nothing." I shrugged.

He leaned into me. "C'mon, own up."

Car ambled over to the scarecrow. "Hey, Preston. What's up?"

Preston jabbed a thumb at me. "Kid's a Sovereign, I think!"

Car adopted a look of exaggerated interest. He glanced at me, and Preston couldn't see his wink. "So?"

"So I wanted to know what he could do, and stuff."

Car put an arm around Preston's shoulders and said to me, "You know what Preston here can do?"

I shrugged, took a swig off my beer, tried to be cool.

All smiles, Car said, "Preston here can get shit-faced and be an asshole, sometimes." He tapped Preston's stomach. "Get some air, man. You're looking green."

Preston looked confused. Car patted him on the head.

"Hey, Car, guess what," Preston said.

Car's smile cooled a little. "What, Preston?"

"Chicken butt!" He slapped Car on the arm and stumbled away.

Lina's scent, baby powder now slightly bitter from alcohol, preceded her. "What's up, kids?" She slinked an arm around my waist and pulled me in.

Car gave me a casual salute. "Just looking after my guests," he said, and turned away with a wave.

Lina nibbled on my ear. I kept an eye on Car, intrigued, despite the trembling chills Lina was sending down my spine. "What's his deal, anyway?"

"Let's go out back; I'll tell you." Her hot breath was like a leash on me. I followed her into the back yard like a puppy.

People laughed, smoked, and drank around a keg. Lina made a face and took my hand. "Over here."

We went around the side of the house. The moment we were out of sight, she pushed me against the wall and kissed me.

While the beer mildly dulled my overachieving senses, it turned my libido way up. We mauled each other for a little while in the semi-darkness.

Lina drawled, "I'm such a bad influence…"

"Well, I'm pretty malleable…"

She reached down. I gasped.

"I don't think so," she said.

I covered her lips with mine and pushed against her hand… and Mel walked up.

"Nate, man, I am really sorry…"

Lina and I disengaged. Her drowsy smile was a sharp contrast to the irritation I felt. "Mel. What."

"You gotta come around front. Jason's gonna rip Byron Teslowski's head off."

"What?" I pushed away from the wall and Lina backed out of my way. "Teslowski's here? Why?"

"C'mon."

I followed Mel through the back yard and into the crowded house, pulling Lina along with her hand in mine. Inside, fifty-odd sets of human scents and the cacophonous punk rock on the stereo assaulted my fuzzy senses. I shook my head rapidly in an attempt to reset. I'd probably need to be sharp.

We went through the front door and on to the lawn. Jason and Teslowski were chest to chest near the curb. A few people stood around and watched with detached amusement, and I was struck by how differently this crowd reacted to a fight, compared to the kids at school.

Teslowski had about a head and a half of height over Jason, but being physically outclassed had never stopped my short-tempered friend before. Jason had no idea of Byron's unique abilities, though, and that made me very nervous.

I crossed the yard with long steps. "Teslowski, what are you doing here?" I hadn't seen him since our meeting on Monday.

Teslowski and Jason turned together. Jason's face was bright red. "He came looking for you, Nate! I told him he'd have to deal with me!"

Teslowski was rigid and pumped. "Tell this little shit to back off, Charters. You know I'll kick his ass."

Threats were a special kind of fuel for Jason. "Fuck you, fucker! I'll tear off your fucking head and shit down your throat! I'll rip out your eyes and piss on your motherfucking brain, ass-hole!"

I heard Lina sigh, "Oh, for crissakes." Peripherally, I saw her cross her arms and shake her head.

I stepped forward with my arms out. "It's cool. Chill out, both of you."

Jason immediately stepped back, but he never took his eyes off of Teslowski, and his fists remained clenched. "Fucker thinks he can come here after you..."

Teslowski rolled his eyes. "If I wanted to kick the shit out of anyone tonight," he said, "I would have started with you."

Jason lunged. My open hand met his chest and held him there. My friend's eyes widened at this reminder of my deceptive strength, and he deflated slightly.

"Dude. You must. Chill." I looked at Teslowski. "Both of you." I took my hand off of Jason and got between them, facing Teslowski.

"What do you want?"

"We seriously need to talk."

Car came out of the house. "What's going on?" He gestured loosely at Teslowski. "Do I know you?"

"Carson Meunetti," I said quickly, "meet Byron Teslowski." They automatically exchanged nods. "He's a… I know him."

Carson looked at the two of us, and Jason. He said to Lina, "Everything cool here?" When she nodded curtly, her lips tight, he shrugged. "Don't kill each other on my lawn. I don't need the police."

He went back inside.

I pointed at Teslowski. "Come on."

TWENTY-EIGHT

Lina turned toward the house. We followed her upstairs to the master bedroom.

The room was perfectly kept up, but smelled of old dust, like it didn't see regular use. Above the king sized bed was a huge, framed photograph of a middle-aged couple I assumed were Car's folks.

I stood by the door. Lina propped herself against a tall chest of drawers. Teslowski sat on the edge of the bed with his hands between his knees. He looked at us.

I nodded. "She knows," I said, "and it's cool. You can trust her."

He paled a little and his eyes went big. "You told her?"

Lina shrugged. "Don't freak out, man."

"Byron, what's going on? How'd you know I was here, anyway?"

"I went by your house. Convinced your mom to tell me."

"Okay… so?"

He squirmed a little. "Remember what I said a few days ago? About watching out for each other?"

"Sure."

"Well, I got called into the principle's office this morning. My parents are there, and Ms. Elp, and this dude from some medical place." He paused to bite at his left index finger. "Fucker said he wanted to talk about my sports."

I didn't get it. "Why?"

"He says he always sees my name in the paper, any time Abbeque Valley wins a game. He's like, 'I wanted to meet the young man who is so good at so many things. '"

I shivered. "You think..?"

"Well, yeah, dude, of course I do! Turns out he's been talking to my parents all week about me doing some survey, or test, or some shit, at this place in Irvine."

Lina tilted her head. "What place?"

Teslowski took off his baseball cap and scratched his head. "Tyndale Labs, or something."

"What kind of survey," I asked.

"Like, a physical, and stuff. He said it was this study on, like, the physical development of adolescents, or whatever. But, no shit, dude, this guy wasn't no doctor. I know it."

I might have been infected by my mother's attitude about this whole thing, but I was certain Teslowski was right. I still tried to sound skeptical. "How would you know, though?"

He shrugged violently, and waves of anxiety rode on his sweat. "Dude, I know it! I've been waiting for something like this to happen."

"Look," I said, "I know you said that on Monday. But why couldn't this guy be legit?"

Lina surprised me. "If he was, why come to the school? Why not just meet you at your house?"

"I guess he was looking at my records," Teslowski said.

I frowned. "Can just anybody do that?"

Lina said, "I don't think so. Not unless his parents okayed it."

"They probably did," Byron said ruefully. "My dad would be into anything to promote my sports. Plus, the guy said he'd pay us."

Lina nodded. "Yeah, like this friend of mine who signed up for all these clinical trials for money. Screwed him up, kinda, too."

Byron frowned at her. "Thanks a lot."

I'd seen so much crap on the news all week, it was way too easy to think the absolute worst. "Forget that," I said. "When do they want you to do this?"

"Next Friday after school," Byron said. "I'm supposed to spend the whole weekend."

I nodded, thinking. "Okay, cool, a whole week. Lina, your dad's, like, a councilman, right?"

"Yeah."

"Could he, maybe, look into this Tyndale Labs place? See if it's legit?"

"I can ask him." She frowned. "He's gonna want to know why, though."

"We can figure that out, I guess. If it turns out to be a real place, then there's no problem, right?"

Byron didn't look so sure. "What if it is? What if it's all some big cover for the government or something?"

Lina tapped her cheek with her index finger. "What if the place is legit, and they do all that stuff with Byron. Won't they figure out he's different anyway?"

That got me. My own doctor had told me my blood chemistry had different levels, and what not, than most folks.

"Hm. Yeah. Probably."

Byron shook his head. I could see the white of his eyes all around his irises. He didn't look like the kid who'd been such a bastard to me all these years. "No way, dude. No way can anyone find out."

I could relate, but I didn't get why he was so scared. "Well, shit… what if you just told your parents you didn't want to go?"

"Not an option," he said flatly. "Not with my dad. I'm going."

We were all quiet.

"Well," I said, and I sounded lame even to myself, "we've got a week, right? We'll figure something out."

Teslowski looked at me. His expression, the tension in his body, the fear and insecurity in his scent was so strong, I had to fight the urge to back into the wall.

"I fucking hope so, dude. I don't want to get experimented on."

I swallowed, tried to pull it together. "Don't worry, man."

I was totally worried, though. If they were sniffing around Abbeque Valley, then did they know about me? I thought about that Preston guy downstairs. Was he really just some drunk punk, or..?

I sighed. This was getting ridiculous. I looked at Lina and Byron. "Let's get out of here, all right? I think I'm over this party."

Byron looked at his digital watch. "I gotta get home anyway."

Lina led us downstairs. On the last step, Byron touched me on the shoulder.

"I, like, owe you, dude."

I didn't know what to say. For a second—just a fraction of a second—I wanted to be totally mean to him. I wanted to shove his nose in all those years he'd been such a bastard to me. For him to be coming to me like I had all the answers, because he knew I was smarter than he was, and I was the only one he knew who had this one crazy thing in common with him… I wanted to be an asshole to him, just once. Finally.

I shrugged off his hand.

"Don't worry about it, Byron."

TWENTY-NINE

Teslowski found his own way out. Lina went to tell Car we were leaving, and I looked for Mel and Jason.

They were talking to a tall blonde guy near the stereo.

"I'm outta here," I said.

Jason frowned. "What's going on with Teslowski, Nate?"

Mel raised an eyebrow and caught my eye. "It's some crazy stuff, Jason," I said. "I'm sorry you got involved."

He shrugged and flashed a feral smile. "No big thing, man—I've been looking for an excuse to call that prick out."

I smiled. "Well... thanks, I guess. But he wasn't looking for trouble." He was bringing it, I thought. "I promise I'll fill you in, but right now, Lina and I are gone. You guys want a ride?"

Mel looked at the blonde guy, who said, "S'cool. I can get you guys home if you need a ride later."

Mel high-fived him. "Thanks, Alex!" He said to me, "Alex is in Carson Meunetti's band."

We shook hands. "How's it going," Alex said.

"It's been a really interesting party," I said.

Lina came up. "Hey, Alex." He nodded to her. "You ready, baby?"

I took her hand. "Yeah."

We went outside and got into her car. Lina gave me a lopsided grin. "So. Hard to top all that." She started the car. "What now?"

I was tired. "Can we get some food? You hungry?"

She glanced at the dashboard digital clock. "It's only eleven. How about I take you back to my place, handsome?"

That provided a little boost to my fading metabolism. "I thought you'd never ask," I mugged. "But... can we make some sandwiches, or something?"

Lina lived in a large house near Abbeque Lake. It was one of the most expensive neighborhoods in town. Her driveway was the size of my front yard.

"Wow."

She smiled and looked away from me for a moment. "Money and politics..."

We went through the front door and into the living room. Two people looked up from a huge television.

"Hello, kids!" Despite the late hour and the bathrobe she wore, the woman's hair and make-up were perfect. She rose smiling, and held out her hand. "I'm Mrs. Porter, Lina's mother. You must be Nathan!"

I shook her hand. "Pleased to meet you, Mrs. Porter."

A young man got off the couch. He looked about my age, but it was hard to be sure. I could see there was something different about him. He stood stiffly, almost at attention.

"Full name!" His voice was slightly slurred, and while he didn't exactly yell, I felt compelled to answer.

"Uh, Nathan Andrew Charters..."

He nodded, a snap of his head. "Six. Equable. Kind. Reliable. Optimistic." He spun on his heel and went back to the television.

Lina took my hand. "That's my brother Tim. He's got a real flair for numerology, that kid..."

Mrs. Porter said, "He's a special boy." She gave me a very direct look.

I nodded. "Nice to meet you, Tim."

Tim shot his hand into the air and let it drop back down.

Lina pulled me away. "We're gonna get a snack in the kitchen, mom."

"All right."

We went through a large dining room and into an expansive, gleaming kitchen. I sat down at a small side table. Lina immediately busied herself putting together some sandwiches.

I didn't know where her head was, but I was a million miles away. My mind raced with what Byron had told us. As much as I tried not to be paranoid, I felt in my gut that Tyndale Labs was up to no good.

I had absolutely no idea what to do about it.

Lina closed the refrigerator and looked at me. "You're all quiet."

"Sorry." I smiled through my nerves. "You've… it's a nice house."

She shrugged and blushed. "We're made of money," she apologized. "There goes my punk rock reputation."

My laugh was almost too weak to fall out of my mouth.

She gave me a shaky look. "What's going on, honey?"

I couldn't remember her ever calling me 'honey,' and we'd only been going out a week. I cradled my head in my hands and sighed before looking up at her.

"I have no idea, at all, what I'm supposed to do for Teslowski," I said. "I'm totally freaked out. All week long, I've been telling my mom to chill out, and now this stuff happens to the only other Sovereign person I know, right here." My voice had an edge of panic in it. I swallowed and got it together.

"I have to do something, right?"

She put a package of deli ham down on the counter, stepped to my side, and kissed the top of my head. "You almost sound like you don't want to."

"No, I do. I mean, I have to, you know?" I shook my head. "Pretty ironic—why couldn't it have been Jason who was the other Sovereign in town?"

She rolled her eyes and laughed. "Oh, sure—the power to… what was it? Tear off people's heads and crap down their throats?"

That made me laugh, and in that laughter, some of the weight fell away. Lina did that, and I felt very grateful for her. I wrapped an arm around her waist and gave her a squeeze.

"We'll sort it out," she said.

I stood up and gave her a quick kiss. It was a little thrill, with her mother and brother right in the other room.

"Thanks for being with me, Lina."

She touched my cheek with her long fingers. "I should thank you, Nathan."

"Huh?"

"You were, like, totally cool with Tim. Totally normal."

"Well, sure." I didn't quite get it. "Why wouldn't I be?"

She put both hands on my shoulders. "Nate, it's tough truth time." The twinkle in her eyes contrasted with her serious tone. "You should know that I've had other boyfriends."

Car Meunetti's face immediately came to mind. I pushed him away and made myself chuckle. "I guess I kinda figured that."

Her mouth twisted. "I'll take that up with you later, Mr. Charters." She took my hands in hers. "Point is, they weren't all so nice to Tim. He's different, y'know?"

I laughed before I could stop myself. "Um, hello? You're going out with the poster boy for different! Who am I to judge?"

I was shocked to see her eyes tear up. "You are amazing, you know that?"

I could feel the heat rise in my face. I shrugged and picked at a bit of stray lunch meat. "I just… you know, I know what it's like, you know? I mean, at least your brother looks normal, right?"

She squeezed my hands. "I know you don't look normal. You're… you fascinate me, Nate. I think you're gorgeous." She kissed me, and wiped her eyes.

"Let's eat."

I was ravenous, and besides, eating would let us both get through the moment we'd just had. We sat down at the table with ham sandwiches and glasses of milk. I threw chunks of food down my throat and finished way before Lina.

I found myself smiling.

"Gorgeous, huh?"

She beamed. "Yup."

"Well." I looked at my plate for some distraction, but I'd cleaned it too well. I managed to meet her eyes. "You should know… I can't believe I'm with anyone so beautiful."

Her eyes sparkled. "Face it, tiger—you hit the jackpot."

I looked back down at the empty plate. "Um… so… your brother. How's he do it, anyway?"

She shrugged. "I don't really know. It used to be that he could just do really quick math, you know, in his head. He's got… he's autistic. Then my mother," she rolled her eyes and made circular motions with her index finger next to her temple, "she got into the whole numerology and astrology thing a couple years ago. Tim just soaked it up. He's got the whole thing memorized."

"That's rad."

She looked wistfully toward the living room. "Yeah. I guess. But, I mean, it would be a whole lot better if he was…" She shook her head. Her mousse was losing some of its strength, and she brushed a few gossamer strands away from her eyes. "I love my brother."

She lightly kicked me under the table. "Besides, kitty cat, doing some tricks with numbers and letters is nothing compared with what you and Byron can do!"

I pursed my lips. "It's a trade-off. I spend a lot of time wishing I didn't look the way I do—not that I don't appreciate your opinion of me, that is."

"Shut up!"

"Seriously, you don't know what it's like! One look at me, and everyone knows I'm different. People always think there's something wrong with me. For all the good it's done me, maybe there is."

She kicked me harder this time. "Ixnay on the elfsay itypay, Nate. Have some perspective."

I nodded, a little ashamed. "Yeah, you're right." At least I had all my faculties, and then some.

"Keep in mind," she added, "that those crazy eyes of yours got this girl's attention in the best possible way. Right?"

I smiled. "And I still can't believe that."

After meeting Tim, I began to understand. Lina didn't seem to have any preconceived notions about people. No prejudice in her, not even the natural amount I thought everyone carried around, including me. I figured that was due to having Tim as a brother. I decided I'd have to find ways to thank him.

"You'd better believe it, Nate," Lina said quietly. "Get used to it. Get used to me."

THIRTY

Over the weekend, I tried to be normal. I slept in, rode my bike, mowed the lawn, read, chatted with Lina and Mel on the phone, watched non-Sovereign stuff on the television when I could find it... but I couldn't get the thing with Byron out of my head. Sunday night I went to bed and stared at the ceiling, still clueless, until I fell asleep.

Monday morning at school, the news of the Sovereign Compromise continued to influence the curriculum in all my classes. Worse, I kept overhearing kids use the word "Sovereign" and my name in the same sentence.

My run-in with Terrance Felder the week before gave me a minor reputation at last. Instead of people openly approaching me out of curiosity, or just to make fun, I had some breathing room. People who would have been casually cruel to me two weeks ago avoided looking at me. Funny thing is, I couldn't decide if I liked that better.

The whole vibe had me more tense than usual at school, and tension makes me burn calories faster. I was trying to stay awake in Mr. Byrd's third period Algebra class when an announcement on the PA system summoned me to the office.

Byrd wrote a hall pass and handed it to me with a mildly curious look. I'd been to the office more in the last few days than in my entire academic career, and my teachers noticed.

Ms. Elp met me outside the office. She put a hand on my shoulder and led me in.

"Nate, there's a gentleman here to see you," she said. "A doctor."

Her hand suddenly felt like a clamp. "A—a doctor?"

But we were in her office. A thin man in a dark suit stood up from his chair and extended a dry, narrow hand. "Nice to meet you, Nate. I'm Doctor Brenhurst. Call me Les."

His small eyes darted with glittering twitches. He was studying me, and unlike most people, did nothing to hide it.

I ignored his hand. "I don't feel sick." It was a lie. My stomach somersaulted in my belly and I was suddenly sweating.

He smiled, thin and quick. "No, of course you don't. No one thinks you are." He gestured to the other chair, and I reluctantly sat. Ms. Elp settled in behind her desk.

"But you are very… interesting," Brenhurst said.

I kept my mouth shut. My legs jumped. I wanted to run.

Brenhurst's smile dropped a notch. "Well. Aren't you curious about yourself, Nate?"

"Why would I be?"

"In light of recent events."

"Like what?"

I played it dumb. Let him fish.

Ms. Elp spoke up. "Your mother will be here soon, Nathan. You might feel more comfortable then."

Brenhurst's smile flattened further. "That's great. She hasn't returned my calls, so I'm looking forward to meeting her. Finally."

I looked out the office window and tried to keep from leaping out of the chair. This guy's been calling the house? Why didn't my mother say anything?

"Well." Brenhurst tapped his knees with the tips of his fingers. For some reason, this very precise gesture scared me. He made me feel like prey.

My mother burst in less than three minutes later. I know this because I watched the clock to avoid looking at Brenhurst.

"What the hell is going on?"

Brenhurst stood up and tried the handshake again. "Mrs. Charters, I'm Les Brenhurst, head of research at Tyndale Labs. I've left you a few messages..."

I watched her pupils dilate and her nostrils flare. "Tyndale Labs, now, is it?" She sneered at him. The cords in her neck stood out.

I looked at Brenhurst. His eyes narrowed, just for a split second, before he forced a laugh and brought his smile back. "Mrs. Charters, if you could..."

He reached out his hand. She jerked away. "Don't touch me." There was a slight tremor in her voice. Her scent carried a powerful mix of anxiety and fearful hate that seemed to be out of proportion, even for this guy. She glared at Ms. Elp.

"I'm taking my son home. We didn't agree to this meeting."

Ms. Elp started to speak, but Brenhurst and my mother dominated the scene. He held up his hands and laughed again in an attempt to be disarming. "I apologize... we only want to help your son."

"He doesn't need your help." My mother took my hand. "Let's go."

THIRTY-ONE

In spite of everything, I was embarrassed. What if anyone saw me? I wanted to escape my mother's grip as she pulled me through the door, but it would have taken the kind of strength that might have hurt her hand. We were out of the school, down the steps, and into the parking lot in seconds.

"Man," I said, "that guy..."

"Not until we're in the car," she snapped.

I shut my mouth. Once we were in the car and she very deliberately locked the doors, I looked at her.

"He had no business," she said. I had a hard time remembering she wasn't angry at me. "I'm tempted to sue the ass off of this school, and that dyke Elp, and Tyndale Labs..."

I found myself defending Ms. Elp. "Well, at least she called you."

She stabbed the key into the ignition and started the car. "This is exactly what we were worried about. Do you see it now?"

She didn't know the half of it. I debated telling her about Byron Teslowski's meeting with Brenhurst last week.

I didn't say anything.

As we pulled onto Abbeque Valley Parkway, my mother said, "I'm taking you out of school." When I gasped, she said, "You can do the same as Lina, do home study."

"But..."

"It's not open to discussion."

I think my indignation was an automatic response. As we drove in silence and I tossed it around in my head, I recognized I didn't mind the idea so much at all. What had going to school ever brought me but unwanted attention, abuse, and grief?

I was a smart kid. I'd end up with a lot more time. And with Lina on home study, too, this might actually have advantages.

As if leaving school would automatically give me a normal life. There was still this Brenhurst guy, and Byron was still going to Tyndale labs on Friday, even if my mother would never let me get into the same predicament.

I looked at her. She still carried the same mix of fear and righteous rage she'd had in Elp's office.

"Mom, what's the deal with that Brenhurst guy?"

"What do you mean?"

My nostrils flared as I tried to gather information from her scent. "I mean, he really pissed you off. Almost like you knew the guy."

"Oh, I know him, all right," she said. "I know the type. Slimy opportunist. A government man if I ever saw one." She looked like she wanted to spit. "And I've seen more than enough."

"Government?"

"Or corporate... it doesn't matter. I'm going to find out what this Tyndale Labs is all about. I'm absolutely making those calls I was thinking about. We'll see what the Sovereign Compromise says about being solicited like this."

I noticed my mother kept changing her mind on the issue of my status. "Um... I thought I wasn't supposed to say I was a Sovereign."

She glared at me. I looked out the window and kept my mouth shut the rest of the way home.

THIRTY-TWO

I jumped on the phone as soon as we got home. Lina answered right away.

"Guess what happened to me today," I said with a touch of sarcasm.

Her voice was light and full of fun. "Um… nope, I don't know."

"Hold on." I put the phone down and did a quick reconnaissance. My mother was in her bedroom and the door was closed. I picked up the receiver and started pacing the kitchen. "Okay. I'm back. I met the guy from Tyndale Labs."

"Shit."

"Yeah, shit. His name's Les Brenhurst, and he called himself a doctor. Said he was, like, head of research, or something."

"Oh my God. Are you all right?"

"Yeah. My mother was called in. I thought she was gonna tear off his head. She was mega-pissed."

"So I guess you won't be joining Byron," she said wryly.

"Byron..! We've gotta do something about Byron."

"Yeah, I guess so. Sorry, baby… this is getting kinda weird."

I sighed. "I liked it better when I just thought my mother was crazy. But that's not all. She's taking me out of school, putting me on home study."

"Wow! We'll get to hang out a lot more, at least."

"Yeah." I wished I could be happier about that, but everything else eclipsed the one little thing that was good about the situation. "Lina, what are we going to do about this? What are we going to do about Byron?"

"Your mom could talk to his folks."

"Yeah… except Byron seemed really freaked about his parents finding out about him. Shit!"

I heard my mother's bedroom door open. "Nathan, I need to use the phone."

"I gotta go," I told Lina. "My mom wants the phone."

"You're kinda freaking out," Lina said. "You want me to come over?"

"Yes. Please."

THIRTY-THREE

I thought my mother was going to jump out of her shoes when the doorbell rang.

"It's just Lina, mom."

"You invited her over here? Tonight?"

She looked confused, not upset. So I acted like it was no big deal. "Yeah."

I opened the door. Lina gave me a hug and had a little wave for my mother. "Hi, Mrs. Charters."

"Hello, Lina." They shook hands. "You might as well call my Lucy."

Lina beamed, eyes wide. "Really? I can?"

"Why not?"

"Wow. Okay."

I still didn't know how to act when the two of them were in the same room. I mean, Lina and I made out and stuff—it was just too weird to have my mother there, and not be on our way somewhere else.

"So… did you want a drink of something?"

"Sure. Whatcha got?"

She followed me into the kitchen. It was a much shorter walk from the living room than at her house.

I opened the fridge. "Um… take a look."

My mother said, "You two can relax—I'm going to use the phone in my bedroom."

That was a relief. "Okay, mom."

We grabbed a couple of sodas, went back into the living room, and sat on the couch. I tilted my head to focus on what was being said in my mother's room.

Lina made goo-goo eyes. "You're adorable when you do that."

"You're adorable when you do everything," I said. "Hold on. Okay. She's on the phone. We can talk."

"You're a handy guy to have around."

I shrugged. "I guess."

"Seems that way to me, anyway." She squeezed my knee. "So tell me about today."

I related the whole encounter with Brenhurst. "And the thing that gets me is just how badly this guy affected my mom. I mean, she's usually, like, all hippie and whatever, but this went beyond that. She wasn't just angry that this guy was, I don't know, violating my civil rights, or whatever. She was mega freaked. I thought she was gonna claw his eyes out."

"No, that's you, hon." I gave her a dirty look and she stuck out her tongue. "So did you ask her about it?"

"She said he was, like, a slimy government man. Talked about how she was going to sue the school and stuff."

Lina frowned. "Government? I thought Tyndale Labs was some corporation."

"I think she just relates all guys in suits with the government. Oh—were you able to find anything out about the place from your dad?"

She rolled her eyes. "I asked him about it, and of course he's like, 'why,' and I'm like, 'I always see them off the freeway, and I just, like wondered.'"

"Off the freeway?"

"Yeah—they've got this big long building off the Bendis Parkway exit on the Five. I see it all the time."

"Oh." Knowing they were right there in plain sight, I didn't know what to think. Which wasn't really all that different than a minute ago. I shrugged.

"Anyway, he said he'd see what he could find out."

My mother came down the hall. "Lina, would you like to stay for dinner?"

Lina grabbed both my hands. I thought she was going to squeal. It made me laugh.

"I'd love to… Lucy!"

My mother tapped her on the shoulder as she went to the kitchen. "Come on, then. You can help me throw something together."

I tried to assist, but the two of them quickly adopted a kind of bee-dance choreography that I only disrupted by cutting in. I sat at the table and mostly watched.

My mother used the time, and dinner, to get to know Lina. At first, it was obvious she was forcing us to keep the conversation away from the day's events, and it was a little strained. But we all went along. I know I just wanted to have a couple hours of normal time.

I found out things, too. Lina's dad was a Republican, but, as my mother put it, Lina seemed to be holding her own. Lina was in a school play in eighth grade—she played Portia in an abridged version of Julius Caesar. If she had to get a real job, she'd be a veterinarian. She liked to hike in the foothills of Saddleback Mountain. My mother left an open invitation to join us at Kirby Lake in the summer.

That sounded great to me.

After dinner, my mother whipped together some instant pudding for dessert. We ended up in the living room to watch the last half hour of the evening news.

They showed William Donner's compound in Montana, which had allowed the media in for the first time. The plan was for it to be the closest thing to an embassy the Sovereign people would have. It would have a hospital, research center, apartments, and even a cable television station. Right now, it was a few pre-fab buildings and Donner's own house.

I watched my mother carefully. She sat silently for a few minutes and then excused herself.

"Back to the phone, I'm afraid."

Alone with Lina, I nodded at the television. "Are you still cool with all of this?"

"I'm still super-cool with you," she said. "But I don't know about this Institute for Sovereign Studies. Wasn't this place the whole reason Donner felt like he had to go public? Weren't the Feds after him, or something?"

"I think so. They were afraid he was, like building an army, or something."

"Hm. I wonder if he is?"

That made me wonder if Reagan was, too. "Hey."

"Yes, dear?" She darted her face centimeters away from mine.

I stole a split-second kiss. "I've been wondering why Brenhurst was so obvious with me."

"How so?"

"Well, with Byron, he was all, 'you're so good with sports,' and all that. With me, he practically laid it all out, telling me how interesting I am, and how I should be interested in myself because of all this stuff going on." I frowned. "He didn't do anything to hide the idea he was curious about me as a Sovereign."

"Makes sense," she said. "I mean, you're always pointing out how you look different, right? Byron just looks like a jock. There's no reason to be all tactful with you."

I nodded slowly. "Right. And there was no way for Brenhurst to have known Byron already figured out he might be a Sovereign."

"Yeah."

I tuned in on the back of the house again. My mother was still on the phone, and being very careful to keep her voice down.

I stood up. "I wanna call Byron. He should know about today."

"Maybe you guys can compare notes."

"Yeah." I paced for a second. "My mother's still on the phone."

"And you don't want to wait, all of a sudden."

I smiled at her. "You're a good girlfriend."

"I didn't do anything," she blushed.

I took a few steps down the hall. “Mom! Lina and I are going for a walk!”

I grabbed her hand and headed for the door. “C’mon. Let’s go before she can put the phone down and try to stop us.”

“My man of action,” Lina purred.

THIRTY-FOUR

It was faster to let Lina drive. We were at Mel's door in three minutes. His dad let us in and we went upstairs to his room, where he surveyed us with a critical eye.

"So." He cracked his knuckles. "What's going on with you two?"

Lina smiled and gave me a squeeze. "Mad scientists are after my man."

Mel saw my own flat smile. "Oh," he said. "Sure. Nate?"

"I need to use your phone," I said.

He sighed and rolled his eyes. "Here I thought you missed me. What's wrong with yours?"

"My mother's on it, and it's really important." I sat down on his bed and reached for the phone.

"You know how to use it," he said. "Be my guest."

I dug into my wallet and pulled out the tattered, folded sheet that held my phone numbers. I still had Byron Teslowski's number from the brief time we had been friends, back in elementary school. It was the first time in years I had dialed it.

It rang four times. An answering machine clicked. I hung up.

"No one home?" Lina asked.

"I didn't want to leave a message."

Mel adopted a bad Peter Lorre hiss. "All right, Nick and Nora—fill me in, or hit the road!"

We did. Mel listened carefully, pestering his whiskers, before he shook his head.

"I think I've said it before, Nate: you're over-reacting. Why should they care about you?" He grinned and looked at me with his head down. "No offense, of course."

"This guy came to Teslowski, and then he came to me," I insisted. "Something is going on."

"Maybe something," he said. "But I doubt it's this conspiracy crap your mother's been crowding into your head." He took my shoulders and gently shook me. "Let me be clear, Nate… you're not important."

I brushed him off. "I hope you get to say 'I told you so.' Believe me. But what are we supposed to do in the mean time? Just let Byron go off to this place? His parents have totally bought into it—they won't protect him like my mother would."

"Protect him from what?" Mel laughed. "Running on a treadmill and having blood drawn?"

"And what do they find from that blood?" I looked at Lina for support, and she nodded. "They figure out he's a Sovereign, and they tell his folks… at least."

"So what?"

I sighed. "I don't know. But he's made it pretty clear he doesn't want his folks to find out."

Lina said, "I think he's maybe an abused child."

We both looked at her.

She shrugged. "Well, look—he's, like, totally freaked out that his parents would find out he's not just a really good jock. He's been this total bully for, like, the majority of his life, or at least since Nate has known him. He's taking it out on people."

It came right out. "Great. So now I have to feel sorry for him for making my life hell."

"Nate!"

I frowned. "Sorry. I know." I picked up the phone and sighed. "Lemme try him again."

Three rings. I started to hang up on the fourth, but my enhanced hearing picked up a tinny, "Hello?"

I brought the receiver back up to my face. "Is Byron there?"

"Speaking."

"Dude! It's Nate Charters."

"Oh. Hey, man…"

"Teslowski, listen. That Brenhurst guy came to see me today."

There was a beat of silence. Then, "Oh."

"Oh?" Something wasn't right. "Dude, this is not good, you know that, right? Something is definitely going on."

I heard voices in the background. A woman asked who was on the phone.

"You can't talk, right?"

"I'll see you at school," he said.

"No—no, you won't." I started to pace. "My mother took me out. We have to talk about this, Byron."

"The park," Teslowski said neutrally. "Four o'clock tomorrow."

"All right."

"I gotta go, dude."

He hung up.

I looked at Lina. "Tomorrow at four. Romita Park."

"Okay."

Mel snorted. "Is this the same kind of talking thing as last time, or are you two going to refrain from kicking the shit out of each other?"

"Mel…"

"I'm just saying."

THIRTY-FIVE

Tuesday dragged.

My mother was out of the house by seven in the morning. Even though I didn't need to get to school, my body sure didn't know. I woke at five AM and couldn't get back to sleep.

I ate breakfast. I took a shower. I read. I straightened up my room, a little.

It was still a long way to four o'clock.

I listened to the radio. I watched television, disinterested until the Phil Donahue Show came on. The theme of the episode was "My Boyfriend Is A Sovereign."

Well, what do you know?

There he was, an actual, real life Sovereign, on television. He looked like he was in his late twenties, maybe. Normal looking guy.

Except his skin came off in long, translucent sheets.

Everybody peels when they get a sunburn. It wasn't like that. It was more like he was shedding. Or molting.

He said it didn't hurt. It just happened, any time he had too much stress. Apparently the new skin underneath was usually a different complexion than the one he'd just lost, so that he almost looked like a different person when it was all over.

Donahue wanted to know if his guest maybe just had a medical condition. The guy had a written statement from some doctor that he was actually changing on a genetic level every time this happened. In a real way, he almost did become a different person.

His girlfriend came on. She wasn't happy—not that he might be a Sovereign; she'd known about his skin thing the whole two years they'd been together. What made her miserable is they were supposed to get married in a couple of months, and she thought he was shedding all the time because of that. She thought he was trying to get out of marrying her by literally turning into someone else.

The guy was a wreck. Every time his girlfriend came down on him, he looked like he was going to sink into his chair. He kept wringing his hands until finally he pulled a whole glove of skin right off. The new skin was olive and smooth.

The audience gasped. He smiled sheepishly and his girlfriend huffed. Donahue dropped his microphone with faux drama.

The whole thing was crazy, but I don't think I moved a muscle while it was on. It fascinated me that this guy was basically normal, he just changed skin when he got uptight. No powers, no useful abilities… just a guy.

I'd been thinking being a Sovereign didn't really change things all that much for me, if all the other Sovereign people could do miracles and fly and whatever. Even Byron had better Sovereign abilities than I did, if he really was able to physically adapt to whatever situation he was in.

Seeing this poor schmuck on television showed me there were misfits among Sovereign, just like there were among normal people.

And if this guy was any example, there were worse misfits than me.

I figured I should feel sorry for the him. And I tried. But he was so pitiful. He just sat there and took it when his fiancé dug into him. He didn't defend himself at all, even when Donahue tried to draw him out. He just sat there while his fiancé basically picked him apart.

I used to think I was supposed to be that kind of victim. Screw that. I didn't want to be passive any more. I didn't want to run away any more.

I bounced on the balls of my feet, impatient to do something. I started to get an idea of what that would be.

THIRTY-SIX

Lina finally arrived, and drove us the short distance to Romita Park. We found Byron slouched at the same table as last time.

"Hey, you got our favorite spot," I said with a weak smile.

Teslowski glowered under the brim of his baseball cap. "Hey." He nodded to Lina. "Hey."

I said, "Lina found out some stuff about Tyndale Labs."

Byron sat up. "Yeah?"

"Yeah," said Lina. "I asked my dad what he knew. Turns out they build, like, medical prosthetics and stuff."

I frowned. "Wooden legs?"

She shrugged and smiled. "Well, I guess. But I guess it's a lot of mechanical stuff." She flexed her arm and made hydraulic noises. "Like the Six Million Dollar Man. You know."

"So what's that have to do with Byron and me?"

"They're a big corporation. They probably do lots of other stuff."

Byron shook his head. "No shit. I knew it. They wanna experiment on us, dude."

"I don't know about that," I said, "but I'm not gonna find out. My mother's not going to deal with them, no way. But you..."

Byron took off his hat. "I'm fucked." He ran his fingers through his short hair. "Game over, man. Game over."

Lina said, “Look, Byron, why don’t you just tell your parents?”

“No way.”

“But why not?”

He held up his hands. “I can’t.”

She crossed her arms. “They’re just your parents—they can’t be worse than that creep Brenhurst.”

“I said I can’t!” He cast his eyes around the grass until he found a small stone, which he snatched up and threw across the field. I mean, all the way across. It went further than my eyes could follow. That’s far.

“I can’t let my dad find out.”

Lina and I exchanged glances. I bit my lip.

“All right, man. It’s cool.” I sighed hard. “You’re not going.”

“How?”

My legs twitched like they had in Ms. Elp’s office. The urge to run. But I wasn’t going to do that any more. This would be more like evasion.

“We’re not going to be here come Friday night.”

I couldn’t help but smile when Lina and Byron provided a stereo “Huh?” I almost said, “Jinx.”

Lina shook her head. “I don’t know if I want to hear this.”

I gave her a kiss on the forehead. “I hope you do—I’m gonna need your help.”

“Dude, you’ve got a plan?”

Barely.

“Sure. We have to get you out of the house before your folks take you to Tyndale.” I scratched rapidly behind my ear. “Hey. Where do you live, anyway?”

“On Santa Salvador. Across from the Glen.”

That helped… so long as the bear-bum wasn’t still hanging out there.

“Cool. When do your parents normally get home?”

“Depends on the day.”

“Thursday.”

“My dad gets home around six. My mom works late.”

“You have any brothers or sisters?”

"No. Why?"

I was thinking at a mental run. "So it's just you and your dad until… when?"

"Ten or eleven." Byron put his hat back on. "Dude, what's this plan?"

I told them. Lina laughed, but she looked at me like I was crazy. Byron smiled, even if it was a thin, desperate thing. I think he was glad to have something to do, some slim hope. We all knew it wouldn't solve anything in the long run, and we'd probably be grounded for life.

We would do it anyway. It would buy us some time to make up the next thing.

I had no idea what the next thing would be.

THIRTY-SEVEN

Lina and I returned to my house. My mother wouldn't be home for another hour or so.

"Nobody home," Lina said. She tickled the back of my neck. "What's on the agenda, kitty cat?"

We kissed just inside the front door. I'd already noticed that Lina's body temperature was a few degrees lower than my own. She was always cool to the touch. Except for her mouth. Her tongue burned across mine, smooth and hot.

She took my hand. "C'mon."

We made it to my bedroom and fell across my twin bed. "How much time..?" she muttered into my ear.

"An hour, I think."

"Okay."

She rolled on top of me and we kissed again. And again. And more. I closed my eyes and away we went.

We'd never been absolutely alone, left to our own desires, as it were, since our first date, and we had a lot less room in her car. We twisted around each other; we pushed against each other. We panted and laughed and guided each other's hands, alternately tentative and eager to feel more. We left each other's faces, ears, and necks slick where our mouths bit and licked and dragged across skin.

Our clothes stayed on, but our grasps and clutches found the flesh underneath. Her fingernails left light scratches along my back that sent electric fissures down my spinal column and through my legs. I realized with sudden, unexplainable guilt that my fingers had found her nipple, but before I could pull away, she placed her hand over mine and squeezed.

I opened my eyes. Her own eyes were hooded and shining. She smiled at me.

I had no words. This wasn't even sex… and that meant sex would be even more unbelievable than this.

She traced my cheek with her free hand and her expression softened. "Lucky me," she whispered.

I just shook my head and laughed. I still couldn't talk, so I kissed her again. She reached down and slipped her thin hand between my pants and my ass.

A clicking, meshing sound, metal moving between metal, broke through the air. I sat up.

"What..?"

"My mother's home."

"Darn it."

We put space between us on the bed. I swung around and put both feet on the ground. Lina found a couple of Rolling Stone magazines next to the bed and threw me one.

We made like we were reading. I was shaking. Her hair was a fiasco.

"Nate?" My mother called out from the living room. "Are you and Lina here?"

We straightened up, brushed ourselves off in a futile attempt to lose the wrinkles in our clothes, and headed out.

My mother put her purse on the couch. "Oh, there you two are. Where'd you go?"

"Uh…" How did she know we'd gone anywhere? "We drove up to Romita for a little while."

"Hm." She looked at both of us, her mouth an even line.

"Lina, your hair is even more messed up than usual." She gestured to the couch, so we sat down. "This is uncomfortable for all of us, children, so I'll only say it this one time, all right?"

I could feel myself turn red.

"When you're in this house," she said, "under this roof, you'll keep it to first base. Understood?"

I was mortified. "Mom!"

"Understood? I want to hear it from both of you, and I expect you to mean it."

"I can't believe..!"

I heard Lina swallow hard. "Yes, Mrs. Charters." She nudged me.

"Understood," I said.

Lina patted my hand. "Well. I guess I'd better go." She smiled, sheepish. "Homework, or something. I've got to do. At home."

"See you again, Lina," my mother said.

"I'll call you," I said.

"Okay." At the door, so close to escape, Lina got some of her nerve back. "Nice to see you, too… Lucy."

She left me there with my mother and my embarrassment.

My mother slapped me on the knee. "Oh, relax, Nathan. I know you two were behaving yourselves, more or less. I just want you to know I'm serious about you keeping it that way."

I shook my head. "You enjoyed that."

She shrugged and smiled. "Mother's prerogative. How are you holding up?"

Oh, mother, if you only knew. "Alright, I guess. I mean, it's only been a day." I smirked. "Not really long enough to miss all the, you know, like, great company and supportive classmates and whatever."

"Especially when there's so much to keep you busy around the house," she said sarcastically.

I turned away. "Yeah…"

"We'll go back on Monday," she continued. "We have an appointment with Mr. Giles to get you set up with home study."

"Okay." Something occurred to me. "I'm not, like, grounded, or anything, am I?"

My mother looked confused. "Why would you be grounded? Just behave yourself with your lady friend, do your studies when you get them, and…" She thought about it. "Actually, it would be good if you maybe did at least lay low for a little while."

"Um…" I thought about my plans for Thursday night. "What does that mean?"

"I'm still not sure what that bastard from Tyndale Labs wants with you."

I started to worry. "So… what does that mean, mom?" I could be grounded for all intents and purposes if she didn't want me to leave the house.

"Just don't announce yourself," she said. "You know what I mean. Stay around the neighborhood." She gave me a semi-serious scowl. "Don't go getting into any fights. How's that for a guide-line?"

I decided this was going to be one of those things where I wouldn't know I'd done something wrong until she told me. "I guess I'll cancel the rest of my grudge matches for the rest of the week," I said.

"Very funny."

She turned on the television and switched channels until she found the news. That reminded me of the talk show.

"Oh hey—I saw this thing today on Donahue. They had a Sovereign guy."

"Really?"

"Yeah." I told her about the man's molting "ability." "They had this idea that he was shedding his skin because he was, like, unhappy with his life. Like he could change things by changing himself."

My mother was suddenly very attentive. It gave me pause. "Um… anyway, it got me thinking."

"About?"

"Well, I've got, like, all these animal-like things I can do, right?"

"I don't know that I would call it that, but all right."

She was getting tense, which made it hard for me to not be uptight. "Well, c'mon—I mean, I can see in the dark, I can smell dinner down the street, etcetera, etcetera… I'm like some big human cat or something."

She turned back to the news. "Is that how you think of it?" She kept her voice light, but what was bothering her now?

I plowed through. "My point is, I don't feel like an animal, or anything, you know? So how is my Sovereign stuff related to my personality?"

She tilted her head and shrugged. "Whatever they said on Donahue isn't necessarily the only answer."

"I guess…"

"There's a lot to figure out," she said. "So long as people like that Brenhurst prick aren't the ones doing the figuring."

Thursday night loomed in my head and I fought to keep the invisible signs of preemptive guilt from my features and voice.

"Yeah. Screw him, right?"

My mother watched the news. Her scent still broadcast odd tension. If Byron freaking out about Brenhurst wasn't enough to convince me I needed to do what we were going to do, my mother's cryptic anxiety about the guy sealed the deal.

"So… have you found out if he broke any laws, coming to the school like that?"

She sighed, quick and impatient. "Let me watch the news and unwind a little while, all right, Nathan? Go take a shower, and we'll talk about it over dinner."

We didn't, though.

THIRTY-EIGHT

Thursday night at last.

Jason answered the door dressed entirely in black, from his shoes to his knit cap. Once we were in Lina's car, he pulled a tin of shoe polish out of his back pocket and started painting his face.

I knew Jason would be into our little mission tonight, but this made me laugh. "Dude. We're not crossing over the Berlin Wall, you know that, right?"

He smiled gleefully. "Might as well do it right, right?"

Lina shook her head. "Fucking 'A-Team.'" She smiled, though. I think she understood why I'd chosen Jason for tonight over Mel.

Lina let us out three doors down from Byron's house. At Jason's insistence, she killed her lights half a block before we got out, and kept them off until she was around the corner.

On the opposite side of the street, a steep hillside loomed in the dark, overgrown with brush, elephant grass, and eucalyptus trees. Jason shook a hang-loose sign at me and disappeared into that darkness.

The street lamp made it close to daylight for me. As I slinked up to the side of Byron's house, I had to remind myself I was much less obvious than I felt. I crouched down beside the rear bumper of Byron's dad's Chevy Dually. I listened, like only I could.

Television sounds. Doors slammed. A large shadow passed inside the living room window, back lit by a flickering television.

I waited.

A commercial played through, and whatever they were watching resumed. I crept to the front door, stabbed the doorbell with my finger, and dashed with all my considerable speed for the cover of the brush across the street.

I saw Byron open the door and look around. I could see his slight smile in the cool porch light. He closed the door. Faintly, I could make out, "Nobody there, dad."

The tang of the eucalyptus made my nose itch. I squeezed my nostrils between my fingers, hard. No sneezing.

I counted to one thousand, slowly. A delicate breeze marked Jason at just about twenty five feet to my right. I smiled. His shoe polish reeked… to me, anyway.

At one thousand and one, I slipped across the street. Again, I stabbed the doorbell. I knew I wouldn't have as much time, so I darted around the side of their house and crouched below a window.

Byron came to the door again. He put on a good effort. "Damn it!" I heard the door close. "Someone's doorbell ditching us, dad."

Anyone could have heard Byron's dad's response. Across the street, even.

"God damn punks! I don't work my ass off all day to put up with this shit! What did you do?"

"Nothing, Dad!"

Lina and I suspected Byron's dad of having a temper. Hearing him blame his kid for an apparently anonymous prank was confirmation.

I counted to two thousand and listened to the sounds inside the house. The television blared on. Someone rustled through the refrigerator. Byron's dad belched wetly.

Two thousand and one. I rang the bell and shot for the cover of the Dually.

Byron's dad threw open the door. "I know you little shits can hear me! You don't want me to kick your asses—and kick them I will!"

He slammed the door.

Across the street, brush rustled, then spat out a palm-sized rock that smacked against the front door. Bullseye, Jason.

I thought the door would come off its hinges when Byron's dad blasted through it. "God damn punks!"

From the darkness across the street, Jason called out in a warbling falsetto, "Oh shithead… !"

Byron's dad stepped away from the porch. He was no more than eight feet from me. I stopped breathing.

Mr. Teslowski was a big man. Wide. Tall. His face was dark red beneath his blonde flat-top. His fists clenched.

"Come down from there, you little shit, or I'll bring you down myself!"

Jason sang, "Ooh, honey! I'm getting hot!"

I had to choke back laughter when Byron's dad actually hawked, spit, and wiped his mouth with the back of his hand before he lumbered across the street. He was playing right along.

Right after taunting Mr. Teslowski, Jason would have made for higher ground and deeper cover. Byron's dad went right up the hill and into the bushes. I shot across the street and headed up the hill to his right. He made so much noise thrashing around and tossing off threats to Jason, I didn't have to be clever about it at all.

I crouched down and closed my eyes for a moment.

The ground was moist through the knees of my jeans. A concrete drainage ditch up the hill carried the sour tint of mildew and moss. The eucalyptus was still strong, but I managed to suppress its impact on the olfactory landscape I was putting together.

Byron's dad smelled like beer, potato chips, sweat, and old farts. No problem keeping track of him, even when he wasn't crashing through the brush and breathing through his mouth. Further along, Jason's shoe polish beacon was sharp and clear.

I took a deep breath, immersing myself in the scentscape of the hillside. I slowly exhaled through pursed lips and opened my eyes with a smile. I felt pretty good.

Jason called, "Lover boy..!" Byron's dad pounded toward the sound of his voice, but I knew Jason moved as soon as he spoke. I crouched on all fours and crept toward Mr. Teslowski, staying a little higher than him on the hillside.

A sharp star of light suddenly appeared. A key-chain flash-light, I think. Perfect. Now, even Jason would be able to keep tabs on Byron's dad. I smiled and moved until I was fifteen feet behind him, just up the hill.

He kept his light trained in the direction of Jason's last catcall, which conveniently blinded him to most everything else. Jason was at the crest of the hill, probably laying prone, commando style, next to a tall stand of elephant grass.

I found a small rock and pitched it in a high arc. It landed just beyond Byron's dad with a satisfying rustle of twigs and leaves.

I heard him bark with satisfaction. He snapped off the little light and did his best to creep toward the source of the sound.

From the top of the hill, Jason warbled, "I'm getting lonely over here, sweetie!"

Byron's dad whirled and almost lost his balance on the slope. "Son of a bitch!"

I decided it was time to contribute to the conversation before he could move.

"Ooh, me too, big man!" Still on all fours, I moved up the hill until I was about sixty feet from Jason.

"You think it's funny, punk?" Mr. Teslowski started crashing toward me.

On the street below, I heard Lina's car pull up to Byron's house. Perfect.

"Hey, I'm gonna get jealous!" Jason's falsetto now came from further down the hill. He had scurried almost to the sidewalk.

"You can't have him." I made kissing sounds and came to my feet. In my normal register, I added, "C'mon, old man. You're never gonna get us both."

I came to my feet and ran along the crest of the hill. Byron's dad did his best to pursue me, but it was no contest, really. I dropped down the far side of the hill and lost myself in the Glen.

Byron's dad gave it up.

There was no sign of the mysterious bear-bum's scent on the wind. I started to think I'd imagined the whole thing. I pushed my unease away and jogged among the trees in high spirits.

I'd had a lot of opportunities to use my "talents" in the last two weeks. There was no denying the temptation of just letting myself be better than normal people. Especially when the normal people were bullies like Byron's dad and Terrance Felder.

It struck me there might be fewer people who thought it was okay to shit on other folks, if there were more people like me out there.

THIRTY-NINE

I emerged from the Glen three blocks away from Byron's house and walked casually down the sidewalk until Lina's car pulled up a few minutes later. I got into the front passenger seat. Byron and Jason were in the back.

Lina gave me a little smile. "All done?"

"I guess so." I squeezed her hand.

Jason slapped me on the shoulder. "Dude, we ran circles around him! That was so rad." In the rear view mirror, I saw him wipe the shoe polish off his face with a threadbare Def Leppard bandanna.

Byron glanced out the window. "What happened with my dad?"

"He gave up," I said. "I guess he went back to your house. He's probably trying to figure out where in the hell you went."

His eyes darted to meet mine in the mirror. He looked nervous. "What now?"

"I'm hungry."

Lina darted over and kissed me on the cheek. "What a shocker."

She drove us to a twenty-four hour place in Belltower Plaza. Byron kept looking at people in the other booths.

"Byron," I said around a mouthful of chicken strip. "Relax."

"Oh, sure."

Jason twisted his mouth and rolled his eyes. "Dude, what's your problem?"

Byron glared at him. "You don't even know, Talbot. So shut up."

Jason shook his head. "Oh. Okay. You're, like, welcome, dude."

Lina gave Jason a glare that made him sulk. "Will you two chill out?" She said to Byron, "My friend Carson is cool. He'll put you up."

"What about his folks?"

"He doesn't have any," Lina said.

Jason's eyebrows went up. "Whoa. Bummer."

Byron's expression was more thoughtful. If I were him, the idea of no parents would probably sound pretty good. No one around to sell him out.

"What happened?"

"Plane crash," Lina said. "Right before his eighteenth birthday." Her eyes fogged for a split second.

I actually remembered it. A passenger jet came down a few miles short of John Wayne Airport, in the athletic field of some high school. I realized she'd known him then; probably been there to help him through it. I thought about the picture over the bed in Carson's house. "Damn. This is really cool of him, then. To get involved."

"He's a sucker for the underdog," Lina said, not unkindly. "Plus, he'll do whatever I ask him to."

My chest tightened. "He will? Why?" I didn't want to sound jealous, and I could hear it coming out, but what was the deal, anyway?

Lina gave me a curious look.

Byron said, "Does he know about the… does he know about me?"

"All I told him was that you needed to lay low for a while," she said to him. "He's taking a risk, too, you know. We're all minors."

Byron squirmed in his seat. "Oh. Yeah. So, he doesn't know about the… you know…"

"What difference does it make? He's not an idiot." She looked at me. "And he's not an asshole, either." She swiveled back to Byron. "You wanna go back home, Byron?"

Byron looked at his chili fries.

"Fuck no."

I stood up and looked at my watch. "Let's go."

FORTY

We drove to Carson's and nobody said much of anything. After the restaurant, there was way too much tension going around.

The flashing lights were obvious before we reached Carson's house.

"Put your head down, Byron."

"What's going on?"

Two police cars were parked at an angle in front of the house. Car stood in his driveway, arms crossed, talking to three uniformed officers. Two other people stood with them. One of them was Byron's dad.

The other person was Doctor Les Brenhurst.

"Fuck."

"What, dude?" Byron started to straighten up. Jason shoved him back down.

We drove right past. Lina kept her eyes on the road. One policeman glanced at our car, then went back to his notebook, dismissing us.

"Okay, Byron." My heart pounded. "You can get up now."

He twisted around to look in the back window. "Oh, what the fuck?"

"Yeah."

"What the fuck am I supposed to do now? We are fucked!"

"Byron…" I tried to keep my voice cool. I actually thought we were pretty well fucked, myself.

"We're fucked! No—I'm fucked! Game over, man! Game over!"

Jason shook his head and smiled. "Shit creek, dude."

Bryon gave Jason a sudden and violent shove. "Fuck off!"

Jason's head bounced off the window of the car door. "Hey! Chill out, fucker!"

"You chill out! You fuck off! I am fucked! I am so fucked!"

Byron's voice cracked. I looked away. He'd given me a lot of shit over the years, but right then, the last thing I wanted to see was Byron Teslowski crying.

Lina sighed. "We have to take Jason home."

Jason rubbed his head. "What did I do?"

I had some idea of where Lina was headed. My stomach tightened.

"That's not it, Jase," I said. "You've got to show up in school tomorrow."

"Well, what about you guys?"

I looked at Lina. She managed a smile, and that stabilized me a little. I made a decision.

"We'll be in Kirby Lake."

FORTY-ONE

After we dropped Jason off, Lina drove back toward my house. She stopped the car a few doors down, around the corner.

"Are you sure about this?"

I was nothing like sure. I was scared. I felt guilty, and I hadn't even done anything. Yet.

"I'm sure," I said. "But you don't have to do anything. You don't have to get into trouble."

She clicked her tongue. "Silly. Who's gonna drive you boys? Hm?"

Byron cleared his throat and I heard him shift in the back seat. "Um… I can drive. I have my learner's."

Lina and I looked at him. His eyes were red and wide. There was a raised welt where he had scratched his cheek wiping away tears.

Lina shook her head. "No thanks, champ. I love my car too much." She grabbed her chin and cracked her neck. "Besides, if I stuck around, I'd have to cover for you guys. Bad enough if anybody asks Jason where we are."

What were the odds of ending up with a girlfriend like that, my first try? She helped me to be brave. I undid my seat belt and stretched in the seat.

"Ready?"

"Yeah."

She gave me a kiss and I got out of the car.

My street was absolutely silent.

At my house, I walked around to the side yard gate. Very slowly, I lifted the latch. I knew from years of automatic use that I needed to very slightly pull on the gate, or the latch would stick. It couldn't stick. I needed no noise.

I opened the gate smoothly, just wide enough to slip through. I was careful to not let it close itself, and rest it carefully against the latch.

I was in my back yard.

Our kitchen had a sliding door that led to the back yard patio. We usually didn't lock it unless we were both going to be gone. There was a chance my mother locked it when she went to bed.

She didn't.

The sliding door was noisy. I had to open it in tiny increments, a few centimeters at a time. Twice, it squeaked on its runners. To me, the sound was loud as a car alarm.

After pretty much forever, the door was open enough for me to slip through.

I was in the kitchen. The digital clock on the stove said 2:08.

I stood still, tried not to breathe, and listened.

The refrigerator hummed. The water heater clicked.

Nothing else.

I stepped into the living room. I felt like that martial arts guy on the old television show, trying to walk across rice paper. It actually helped me think about how to place my feet. I tried to be aware of my every step.

I found myself wishing I could do this barefoot, but decided against taking off my shoes. No time.

I moved down the hall toward my mother's bedroom. I took a step, stopped, listened, took another step. I breathed through my nose, but kept my mouth open to take in as many scents as possible.

Took another step.

My mother was asleep. I could hear her breathing, shallow and regular.

I was outside her bedroom door. She had left it cracked open. That was a freebie—I wouldn't have to turn the doorknob and worry about the click of the latch.

She was still asleep.

I pushed the door further open and stepped into her bedroom. The pounding of my heart threatened to drown out all other sounds. I was shaking.

Tough to calm down. I'd never broken into my own house before. I'd certainly never stolen anything from my mother, let alone the keys to our cabin. I'd absolutely never run away from home with my girlfriend and the neighborhood Sovereign kid.

I hated this. I thought I was done running.

I closed my eyes and told myself to calm down. I opened my eyes and took another step into the bedroom.

My mother's purse was on the top of her dresser, across from the foot of her bed. It was open.

I glanced at my mother. She was on her side, facing away from me, toward the window.

She was still asleep.

This was going to be the hard part. How on earth could I take out her keys without making noise?

I figured out that one pretty quickly, and just lifted the whole purse. Once I had it in my hands, I couldn't move fast enough. It was torturous to keep cool as I backtracked to the kitchen table. I forced myself to stop twice, listen, sniff.

My mother was still asleep.

In the kitchen, I carefully pulled her keys out of the purse. The keys to the cabin were on a separate ring, a clip-on, attached to her house and work and car keys. That was lucky.

I unclipped the cabin keys and put the rest back in the purse.

It took me a minute to decide if I should return the purse to her bedroom. I decided it wouldn't matter. She'd know I was gone in a few hours. It wouldn't be all that much longer before she figured out where I was, and that was okay. In fact, I was counting on it. Where I left the purse wasn't going to make that much of a difference.

It took longer to get past the rush of indecision I suddenly felt. Why not just wake her up and tell her what was going on? Wouldn't she help? Didn't she hate that Brenhurst guy, for whatever reason?

I turned and looked down the hall. Listened. Sniffed.

My mother was still asleep.

It could have gone either way, I guess. I still don't know why I decided to leave. That's just how it went.

I got out of the kitchen, onto the patio, through the side gate, and back to Lina's car in a careful hurry.

I closed the car door and let out a rushing sigh. Lina asked me if I had the keys.

I nodded. "Let's go."

I felt like I was leaving forever. I was exhausted. I felt like I'd stolen from myself.

"You okay?"

"Don't wanna talk. Let's go."

Lina started the car and headed for the mountains.

FORTY-TWO

Lina drove straight through, sometimes twisting the radio dials or popping Bauhaus and Echo and the Bunnymen tapes in and quietly singing along to stay awake. Byron slept most of the way. We got to Kirby Lake just as dawn made headlights unnecessary.

I was numb with exhaustion, but I don't remember sleeping at all. I stared out the window and fought anxiety. I let Lina hold my hand now and then.

I wasn't mad at anyone, at least not anyone in the car, except, of course, myself. I was sure the whole thing was a mistake, a made-up drama that could have been resolved if we'd just been up front with my mother, and maybe with Lina's folks.

I just didn't trust them. I didn't trust anyone but Lina.

Byron snored in the back seat. Circumstance had closed his own circle of trust down to the freak in the front seat, the very same misfit he'd spent the last few years tormenting.

Maybe my strongest Sovereign ability was the talent to attract irony.

I gave Lina brief directions to my grandmother's cabin. The car's tires ground over the gravel driveway and Byron woke up.

"We here..?"

I undid my seat belt. "Yeah. Rise and shine."

I started to get out of the car. Lina stopped me with her fingers on my shoulder. I turned to her.

She gave me a kiss.

"Good morning, Nathan." She smiled at me, and I felt stronger. Stronger to the point of tears.

"Good morning," I said. I kissed her back and whispered, "Thank you," when our lips were just parted.

"De nada," she said.

We got out of the car. I ached from fatigue and inactivity. Byron stood beside me and took in the scenery.

The air was crisp, but warmer than when my mother and I had visited. The tall pines talked to each other in the breeze, with a birdsong counterpoint.

"Nice up here," he said. His voice was thick, like he was still asleep. He rubbed his eyes.

I nodded. "Out of the way."

I took my mother's keys, unlocked the cabin, and we went inside. It had only been a couple of weeks since my mother and I had been there, but there was still that smell of dust and the stale hint that people had been absent, but their essences remained, fading.

It was a comfortable smell.

Lina put her arm around my waist. "This is cool," she said, taking in the wood paneling and my grandmother's outdated decorating sensibilities. "Cozy. You spend a lot of time here?"

"Summertime, when I was little, mostly. Not that much the last few years." I felt like I was wrapped in gauze. I was so tired. "My dad came here with his folks the whole time he was growing up. I think my parents met up here."

She pulled me closer. "How perfect."

Byron called from the kitchen. "Not much food."

We joined him. He was opening cabinets. There were canned goods, soups and baked beans, mostly, and some powdered milk. Lina opened the fridge. "There's some bottled water and, like, a six-pack of sodas in here."

"We weren't here long enough, last time, to go to the store." I shrugged, and the room didn't keep up with the movement of my head. "Aren't you guys tired?"

"Not like you." Lina appraised me. "But we should eat. You should eat. Then we can sleep."

I dropped into a chair at the small kitchen table. "Okay."

Lina appointed herself cook. In a few minutes we had plates of baked beans and cans of cola on the table. Since food was in front of me, I ate.

Byron said, "I can't believe that Brenhurst guy was waiting for us. How'd he know?"

"No kidding," I said. "That was too weird. Fucking weird."

Lina said, "Proves it, though. Tyndale Labs is up to something with you guys. With Sovereign."

"What was he doing with all those cops there?" Byron shook his head.

"Your dad could have called them," I said. "We pissed him off, royally."

"Not hard to do, dude."

"I figure."

"What's your mom gonna do when she finds out that you're gone?"

I swallowed. My stomach tightened around the food. "She'll call here. She'll know, right off. It's why she brought me up here in the first place, when Donner made his announcement."

Lina said, "Even if your dad called the police, why would he call Brenhurst, too?"

We just looked at her.

"Fuck," said Byron.

"Yeah," said Lina. "Exactly."

"So the police called Brenhurst, or something?" I couldn't figure it out. I was so tired.

Lina shook her head. "I don't know. It's just too much of a coincidence. Too weird." She smiled slightly. "Carson must have been freaked."

Lines creased Byron's forehead and his eyes squinted. "So, why didn't we just stay at your place, dude?"

I reddened, suddenly angry. "I did the best thing I could think of, Teslowski, all right? I figured we'd better get as far away from shit as we could, and you were too busy freaking out to be any help, remember?"

Byron held up a hand. "Dude, I know. I'm sorry. I was… I…" He slumped in his chair and looked me in the eye. "Thanks, Nate. Really."

I sighed. "Okay."

The three of us sat there for a minute.

Lina said, "So what'll your mom do?"

I smiled and stared into the middle distance. "She'll hit the roof. She'll kick ass."

"I don't know what my folks are gonna do," Byron mumbled.

"She'll convince them," I said. "She'll make them feel guilty for trying to turn you over to that place."

Byron let out a long breath. "This is so fucked up."

"Yup."

We sat around the table and thought our own tired thoughts. Finally, Lina said, "Sack time, gentlemen." She stood up, took my hands, and dragged me to my feet. "C'mon. We have a few hours before your mother wakes up and this whole thing gets started."

FORTY-THREE

Lina and I were a hundred miles away from our parents, in bed, together. We had to at least try to mess around, but I was just too tired to get serious. I fell asleep with her head on my shoulder. Her hair tickled my cheek.

I didn't dream. I was awake, I was asleep, and then, I was awake again.

Lina was not in the bed. She was somewhere else in the cabin, and she was screaming.

I shot from the bed, my nostrils filled with the pungent, wild scent I last experienced in the Glen. I couldn't find the owner, then. Now, whatever it was, it was in the house.

I almost collided with Byron in the hall. Together, we came into the living room.

Lina had her back against the wall to my left. She kept her eyes on the bestial figure crouched just inside the half-open front door.

At first, I thought he was some kind of mountain bum, a homeless person who scavenged the dumpsters and lived off charity. His hair and beard were long, overgrown, and matted. His sweatshirt was torn and soiled, his pants ragged and stained.

He didn't have any shoes on. His filthy bare feet were almost furry, with long, jagged, black toenails.

He stood ready to fight or fly, bent at the elbows and knees. His fingers were curved into claws, accentuated by long, black fingernails.

His eyes caught the ambient light of the room, and glowed.

Just like mine.

Byron and I positioned ourselves between the intruder and Lina. I found myself in the same stance as the ragged stranger. I was a cleaner, thinner, younger mirror.

He met my eyes. His pupils were huge, and noticeably oval. His lips curled to reveal pointed, brown teeth. Smile or grimace, I couldn't tell.

"You little rats wouldn't stand a chance," he rasped. "Good thing I'm not here to fight."

His scent choked me. I tried to break it down, control it. Old meat. Dirt. Gravel. Blood. Urine. Animal spoor. Under all that, deep in the foundation that was his sweat and pheromones, was something familiar.

I tried not to hyperventilate. Something was wrong here, worse than some crazy homeless guy breaking in on us.

"What do you want?" My legs jumped with tension.

He licked his lips with a black tongue and asked his own question. "What're you doing here? Not your place, is it?" He looked at me and his eyes literally flashed. "Or is it?"

Byron took a step forward. "He's just some bum." He bunched his fists. "You better clear out, old man."

The intruder made a sound that was half laughter, half bark, and feigned a lunge at Byron. "You don't live here!"

I held up a hand to hold Byron back. I kept my eyes on the stranger. "I do. I live here."

He nodded and snorted. His nostrils and moustache were moist with snot. "I know it. But not now, eh? Not without your mother!" His eyes twitched, nervous and fast, to take in Lina. "Up here for a little fun? Playin' hooky, eh?"

His stench made my eyes water. My throat was tight. I stepped up to him.

"Nate…" Despite his bravado, Byron's tone was cautious.

My face was inches from the bigger man's. His alien eyes never left mind. He trembled.

We were nose to nose. The room shrank down. It was just me. And him.

I opened my mouth, and sniffed.

And I knew.

I think I made some kind of noise. Maybe it was a sob. Maybe I was just gagging on his scent, so harsh, and so much like my own.

I stumbled back. I think Byron had a hand on my arm. Lina was next to me. I couldn't see anything but him.

Everything was over. Everything I knew, everything that made up my life up to that point, was over.

I shook violently. Tears coursed down my cheeks.

"You *fucker*!"

He nodded and smiled, his thick, pointed teeth gleaming in the wiry fur of his beard.

"That's my boy!"

I leapt for him. Byron had my arm.

"Nate…"

I shook him off. "Fucker! Fucker!"

Lina touched my shoulder. "Nate." I actually snapped at her. I growled like a cornered dog.

She didn't even blink.

"Nate." She had her hand on my shoulder, and she squeezed.

Another sob burst from my chest.

My father just stood there. That bestial smile was gone. He crossed his arms over his chest. His head tilted slightly, appraising.

Lina's other hand was on the back of my neck, stroking. She addressed my father, angry, scolding.

"He didn't even know you were alive."

He chuckled. "I knew about him! I've seen him! Watched him!"

The strength washed from my limbs. I think I was in shock. I swayed against Lina.

"You were there in the Glen," I said.

He nodded. "Saw you last time you came up here with… with her. With your… with your mother. Came down to see you some more." He laughed again, a short, sharp vocal burst. "You're my son."

I could barely get the words through my lips. The world felt far away. "You're supposed to be dead."

"I was. I was?" His eyes were bright, like he was enjoying some private joke. Or maybe he was just crazy.

"I was," he repeated. "I am. That guy's dead. I'm not that. Nobody knows, 'pert near. Nobody found me 'cept I wanted them to."

He rocked on the balls of his encrusted feet. His arms swung at his sides. He shook his head back and forth. "Wanted to see you."

My father wanted to see me.

I wiped my eyes and looked at him. "Why'd you wait? Why'd you make us think you were dead?"

His eyes lost their shine. He looked away from me. "Not the same… world. Slower. Harder. You… and her, you wouldn't…" His head tilted sharply. "Never said I was dead, exactly. Denver can tell you."

"Denver…"

Denver Colorado, who called my father "that old spook."

The floor felt like it was moving. I reached and found that Lina was still standing there, right next to me, ready. Her solid support made me want to cry again. I found her hand with mine.

"What happened to you? My mother thinks you died in a fire."

He flared his nostrils and rolled his eyes. "Fire? What fire? There wasn't a fire… more like that's what she told you."

My mind raced. "What are you talking about."

His lips snapped away from his teeth and his eyes went wide before he crouched and looked away from me. "I don't know. How would I know? I've been away."

I shook my head. "No. You do know." I felt cold. "She's known. All this time, she's known you were alive. Like this."

He straightened out and puffed up his chest. "Whaddaya mean, like this? You think there's something wrong with me?"

How could I? He was me, but… undiluted.

"No," I said quietly.

"But there is, though." His eyes narrowed. He scratched with his left hand deep into his beard. "I'm too much me." His gaze filmed over for a moment. He coughed a laugh.

I said it again. "She's known, hasn't she?"

He shrugged. "Can't say what she's known or hasn't known. I left right after you were born." Again with the wet laugh. "I heard you had a pelt!" He shook his head. "I guess you shed, eh?"

"My mother told me you died in an explosion, right after I was born. That you never got to see me."

His expression darkened. "No explosion. Nothing to explode, out there! I just left. Had to. She… Lucy… made that up."

I thought I'd feel something more, right then. My father was standing in front of me. He was alive. And he was telling me, in essence, that my mother had lied to me my entire life.

I felt nothing. I guess that was something, right there.

"My mother. She knew you were like this?"

"Yeah, sure." Before he could say something else, he tilted his head back, sniffed, and ducked away from the door.

I heard the car engine a moment later.

Byron said, "What's up?"

"Car coming."

"Your mother?" Lina asked.

My father jerked and his eyes flashed. Apparently he wasn't ready to see her just yet. But I sniffed and said, "No. It's not her car. Someone else."

I pulled the front drapes back just far enough to see a black sedan pull into the driveway. Its windows were opaque.

My father made a noise that couldn't come out of a human throat.

The driver's door opened and a big guy in a dark suit got out. He wore sunglasses and had a blonde buzz cut. The front passenger door opened and his redheaded twin got out. The second man cracked his knuckles and absently patted the bulge under his jacket.

"Who the fuck..?" Byron stood next to me.

The back passenger door opened.

Doctor Brenhurst got out of the car. He pulled my mother out a second later.

Byron almost knocked me over getting away from the window. I stared in shock and spoke to the man who shared my Sovereign genes.

"Do you know the man with my mother?"

He didn't want to look out the window. He acted like a cornered animal. Maybe that's what we were.

"Look, dammit!"

He didn't have to. His sense of smell was probably many times more sensitive than mine.

"That's Lester." His tone was somewhere between hysterical and defiant.

Lina said, "Shit. Makes sense."

I stepped away from the window and went to the door. Everything was coming together. Everyone was here.

"Come on," I said. I swallowed hard and opened the door.

FORTY-FOUR

As soon as I stepped outside, the sunglasses duo took up positions on either side of Brenhurst and my mother. She tried to twist out of Brenhurst's grip when she saw me, but he was strong for such a wraith of a man.

"Nathan!"

There she was, held captive, apparently dragged here against her will, and all I could see was the woman who had made my whole life some kind of story. I turned my attention to Brenhurst.

"Can I help you, Doctor Brenhurst?" My anger gave me the strength to at least sound glib.

"Ah. Nathan. Yes you can."

Lina and Byron came out and stood behind me. Brenhurst smiled. "And your friends are here, too. I was hoping to find Mister Teslowski, at least." He nodded to Byron. "Your parents are very concerned."

Byron's response held just the slightest tremor. "Fuck you."

Brenhurst shrugged. "I need the three of you to come with us. Now."

My mother tried again to pull away from Brenhurst. "Don't listen to this bastard, Nathan."

I stepped off the small wooden porch. "Let my mother go." I sniffed. Where was my father?

The two bruisers each took a single step forward. One of them took off his jacket. His shoulder holster was conspicuous. "Permission to activate," he said.

"No," Brenhurst said quickly. "Nathan. Please be reasonable. There's no need to create any trouble."

"Byron," I said. I was slightly surprised, and very relieved, when he stepped up and stood by my side.

"Which one you want?" I could smell his adrenaline, almost overpowered by his fear, but there he was.

Where was my father?

The other big guy took off his jacket. "Stay where you are."

We were separated by about fifteen feet. I knew I could close the distance with a leap. I was pretty sure Byron could, too.

I was shaking. I don't know if I was scared. I couldn't feel anything but rage. I wanted to feel blood on my hands. My fingers curled into rigid hooks. My legs twitched, eager to move.

"You know what we can do, Brenhurst," I said. "That's the whole point, right? You knew the father, now you want the son."

I saw my mother go pale.

Okay. She knew. Fine.

Brenhurst's face contorted with interest he couldn't conceal. "What do you know about your father, Nathan?"

I didn't get the chance to answer. Andrew Charters burst from the side of the house. He leapt—it was like he was flying—thirty feet at least. He slammed into the blonde bruiser and they slid, hard, through the gravel.

The redheaded bruiser pulled his gun. I'd never seen a real gun before. I froze.

Byron was a blur past me, unnaturally fast.

I heard Brenhurst yell, "Activate!"

My father rolled on the ground with his opponent, snarling and spitting. Byron grappled with the other one for possession of the gun. An actual gun that would probably kill one of us.

Lina yelled, "Nate!"

I snapped out of it and went for Brenhurst. He tried to back away from me. I relished the naked panic on his face, right before

I slashed it with my curved fingers. He grunted and released my mother.

I took her arm and practically threw her toward the house, where Lina took hold of her.

I looked back at Brenhurst. He wiped blood from three angry lines across his cheek. He didn't seem scared any more, only winded.

"Well," he said. "Family reunion."

I took him by the throat. His pulse beat against my palm. "Call them off. Make 'em stop."

His hands automatically came to his neck, and he tried fruitlessly to peel my fingers loose.

"Call them off!"

He shook his head, as much as he could. He looked over my shoulder and smiled.

I lifted Brenhurst by his neck and turned us both around in time to see Byron fly away from his opponent. He'd been thrown. Blood followed him through the air like the tail of a kite.

The bruiser he'd fought rolled his neck like he was trying to loosen a kink. He walked over to the tangled mess of limbs that was his partner and my father and almost casually separated them. He tossed my father away with the hand that wasn't holding the gun.

My father twisted in the air, hit the ground on all fours, and shook his head. His hands and face were sticky with bloody dirt.

A wet, cracking sound brought my attention back to the bruisers. Something was happening to them.

Their clothes shredded. Hard, black, curving spikes, wet and shining, emerged from raw slits in their shoulders, elbows, knuckles, and knees. They weren't wearing these weapons. They were growing them.

I saw by the broad smiles on their faces that this was not happening to them, so much as they were making it happen.

Permission to activate, the one had said.

They faced me, bristling.

"Release Doctor Brenhurst. Now."

I threw Brenhurst to the ground and leapt back. I admit it, all I wanted to do was get some space between me and them. The freak was freaked out.

Brenhurst stood up. He coughed and rubbed his throat. "Get the woman!"

Redhead freak—the one with the gun—ran for the cabin. Lina and my mother were inside. I started after him, but blonde freak stepped in front of me, a wall of spikes and horns. He stank of open wounds.

"Nope," he said.

It didn't matter. My father tackled the redhead around the waist.

Blonde grabbed me by the wrist. "It's over, kid."

There weren't any thorns coming out of his chest. I hit him there with my free hand, as hard as I could.

He let me do it three more times before he twisted my arm behind my back and pivoted me. I felt the spikes on his knees press against my legs. He grabbed my flailing free hand with no problem, and that was that. If I struggled, he'd break my arm, dislocate my shoulder, or maybe rip the limb right off.

Brenhurst put his face in front of mine. My mouth was too dry to spit, or I would have.

"Hold him," he said to blonde.

"Put him in the car?"

"Did I say that?" Brenhurst shook his head and went for the cabin.

Blonde turned us around to face the cabin. My father and the redheaded freak still fought. The redhead had hold of my father's wrists and lifted his arms over his head. Black horns sprouted from the redheaded freak's forehead. Blood from the wounds dribbled down his cheeks.

Held suspended, my father's chest and belly were exposed and vulnerable. His feet jerked, a foot above the ground.

Each toe ended in a curved black claw. If he was a first-generation version of me, and my fingernails had been enough to slice Byron…

My captor must have had something like the same idea. "Earl! The feet!"

The redheaded freak looked down in time to see my father kick up with both hairy, filthy feet.

Earl screamed. It was the most hopeless sound I've ever heard. He dropped my father and doubled over.

His insides fell out. The air filled with the smell of blood and new shit.

Bile exploded in my mouth and my stomach convulsed. My vision blurred with tears.

Blonde's grip on me faltered.

My father grabbed Earl by the hair and lifted up his head. Earl wouldn't let go of his gut, as if he could hold himself together. Grey intestines tangled on his thorned knuckles.

My father leaned in and ripped out Earl's throat. With his teeth. Blood fountained.

Blonde tossed me aside to go for my father. I hit the gravel and rolled, stunned. Bile choked my throat and burned my mouth when I spit. I fought to keep down baked beans and soda.

I could hear sirens. I shook my head rapidly, but the sound was still there, faint, but getting louder. We were going to have help. The thought made me weak with relief.

I stumbled to my feet. My father and the blonde freak squared off in front of the cabin. Byron was still on the ground, out cold. There was blood on the gravel all around him.

Panting, I moved toward the cabin. My mother and Lina were still in there with Brenhurst.

The front door flew open. Brenhurst pushed Lina and my mother ahead of him. He had a gun in his hand. Another gun.

"That's enough!" Brenhurst pushed the gun into the back of my mother's head. She jerked forward at the contact, and she closed her eyes. When she opened them, they shined with rage and fear.

Lina said, "Nate… !" Her own eyes were wild, panicked.

Brenhurst moved the gun to her.

"That is enough!" He looked past them to Earl's body. "Jesus Christ! Charters, you damn fool."

My father just grinned. He and the blonde continued to circle each other.

Blonde grew his own devil horns. "I can finish this one," he said. "I can finish him."

The other gun was on the ground, next to Earl's steaming, ravaged body.

The sirens were louder. I could tell everyone could hear them, now. The sound was painful, even if it did signal salvation.

Brenhurst shook his head. "No. Stand down." When he looked at the blonde freak, I stepped closer to the gun on the ground. "And Charters, if you make a move, I will kill one of these women."

My father didn't take his eyes off the blonde freak. He licked the blood off his lips, but his beard was soaked. He chuckled. "Which one?"

"That depends on which Charters moves," Brenhurst said. "Don't think about that gun, Nathan."

I stopped breathing.

"The police will be here in a few minutes," my mother said. "Are you going to kill us all before then?"

Brenhurst ignored her. "Agent Turban. Deactivate."

My father laughed. "Yeah. Turn it off, and watch what happens."

Agent Turban blinked, but he followed orders. His thorns retracted with slick sucking sounds.

"Don't forget, Andrew," Brenhurst said. "Move and someone dies."

"Someone's gonna die anyway." My father laughed again, looked at me, and shrugged.

I didn't get it.

Brenhurst's voice was low. "You're still in there, aren't you, Andrew. Still brilliant despite the augmentation."

"Comes and goes," my father said. "Lots of noise."

Brenhurst stepped past my mother and Lina. He walked right up to my father. He kept the gun trained on him, but his arm was more relaxed.

They stood there, looking at each other.

I started breathing again and took one more step toward that gun on the ground. I was tired and hurt, but I could have it in my hand in less than a second.

What would I do with it?

"Are you ready?" Brenhurst asked my father.

I stopped.

"Wait. What? Ready for what?"

Brenhurst reached into his pants pocket and pulled out a small black box the size of a garage door opener. It had one grey button.

"Ready to rest," Brenhurst said.

Agent Turban's eyes went wide. "Hey, wait a minute..!"

The police were seconds away. Brenhurst pressed the button.

I could hear the police cars on the street and the driveway behind me, but I couldn't turn around. I couldn't take my eyes off Turban.

He screamed and began to come apart.

It started at his extremities—his hands shook spasmodically. His whole body went rigid. Finally, his fingers just... *disintegrated* in a bloody haze of flesh and bone.

The effect followed up his arms, and his legs. It was as if a swarm of invisible insects was eating him alive, until he was a limbless torso on the ground. He kept screaming until whatever was destroying him reached his chest and vaporized muscle, organs, and bone.

There was no time to register the horror I'd just seen. Behind me, a voice full of fear and revulsion said, "Drop the gun! Everyone, hands in the air, now!"

Brenhurst dropped his gun and turned to my father.

Only, my father wasn't there.

Despite Lina's hysterical crying, despite the puddle of gore that had stopped being a person at the push of a button, despite the police officers rushing us with their guns drawn, I kept my eyes on Brenhurst's face. I saw his astonishment change to fury, then soften to a kind of resignation.

A policeman knocked me off my feet. I felt the cold metal of handcuffs on my wrists. My face was in the gravel. So I can't say for sure if I saw Brenhurst smile.

FORTY-FIVE

It's hard to put it all together, in order.

Here's what happened.

The cabin was a crime scene. There were two dead bodies there, or at least what was left of them. Brenhurst pinned the deaths of his two bruisers on Andrew Charters, who he claimed was a dangerous rogue Sovereign. He accused my mother of concealing my father's whereabouts.

Since the Sixties.

Of course, my mother wanted to press charges against Brenhurst for kidnapping, assault, and attempted murder. The last was for Byron, who was taken away in an ambulance. And for my father.

The cops had enough evidence to book Brenhurst, but he wasn't held. He had friends in high places, it seemed.

We had friends, too. Lina spoke to her parents, who drove to Kirby Lake to get her back. The councilman and his wife, thankfully, believed their daughter, and my mother.

I watched Brenhurst leave the police station, and he knew it, but he never even looked at me. He carried himself like he'd just paid a parking ticket.

That was the moment I decided he wasn't my enemy. I was his. I told myself I wouldn't let him get away with any of this.

Right before Lina left with her parents, we had a few seconds. She gave me a crooked smile, but her eyes were puffy and bloodshot.

"I'm sorry," I whispered. I wanted to cry, seeing her so drained. The things she'd been through in the last two weeks. The things she'd seen, just that day. Because of me.

She shook her head and tried to laugh, but it turned into a little choked sob. She held it together and wiped her eyes.

"I love you," she whispered. That was just about the worst thing of all… that I heard her say those amazing words under the most awful circumstances.

Everyone was all around, so we gave each other a hug that felt awkward and inadequate, and she left with her parents.

It was just me and my mother, then. Denver Colorado was coming for us in a few minutes. We sat next to each other on a wooden bench.

"Nate," she said. It was the first time she'd been able to directly address me since she'd stepped out of Brenhurst's car.

I closed my eyes. I was so tired.

"Mom. I don't want to talk about it."

"I want you to know…"

"Mom." I opened my eyes, but I couldn't look at her. Not yet.

She didn't say another word until Denver arrived.

FORTY-SIX

Denver drove us home in his modified Ford Econoline van. There was plenty of time to talk, but I kept my mouth shut. I was just too angry. My mother, and this guy…

I remembered the way he'd stared at me when we first met, a little over two weeks ago. At the time, I thought it was just the typical reaction most people have. Now I knew he had recognized me, or maybe the family resemblance.

He and my mother barely talked. The silence, and the gently jostling van, forced much-needed sleep upon me.

I woke up shortly before we pulled into my driveway. I slid open the side door of the van and let myself into the house. Outside, I heard my mother help Denver with his chair.

I looked around. I hadn't been gone even twenty four hours, but enough had happened in that time, I didn't even feel at home in my own living room.

Denver used his tremendous upper-body strength to roll his chair over the front stoop and into the house. My mother followed.

"So, Nate," he said. "I guess you want to talk about all this."

From his tone, you'd think he was inviting me to tell him how school was going. I scowled.

"I think I know enough," I said, even though I did want the whole story. I wanted to know exactly how badly I'd been lied to by my own mother.

She squeezed past Denver and went into the kitchen. She didn't look at me. I barely looked at her.

Denver rolled next to the couch, gestured for me to sit down. I crossed my arms and stared at him.

"Suit yourself," he shrugged. He called into the kitchen. "Lucy. I'll wait for you."

My mother came into the living room with three glasses of ice water. She held one out for me. "Table's fine," I said. She lowered her eyes and set my glass on a coaster on the coffee table.

Denver took his glass. My mother sat on the couch next to his chair.

I said, "Well? You two want to get it off your chests? Make yourselves feel better?"

My mother's face finally moved from slack shame to angry color. "Nathan, that's enough. You have no idea of the situation."

"No kidding."

My mother and Denver exchanged glances. Denver began.

"I met your father when we were both teenagers," he said. "When his folks would come up to Kirby Lake. We hit it off, stayed in touch over the years."

"I met Denver the first time Andrew took me to the cabin," my mother said.

"Right. Once your mom and dad got married, they didn't come up all that often, but we still kept in touch. Your dad is... well, he was a brilliant scientist, Nate. He worked for the government on some stuff, but he couldn't tell us about it."

My mother inclined her head. "Well. He told me enough. They called it Project: Rancher."

"What was that?" Despite my desire to remain stubbornly uptight, I was quickly fascinated. This was it. The story of my father. The truth. I sat down on the other couch.

My mother said, "They had a way to change people's bodies using very small... machines. They could make improvements, add things… your father thought the machines could be used like medicine. Cure cancer, or even slow down the aging process."

"You're serious."

My mother nodded. "The operation was administered by a man I never met in person, not until a few days ago."

"Brenhurst."

"Right."

I shook my head, anger flaring fresh. "If you knew who he was…" I thought about the last twenty four hours. I thought about Byron in a hospital somewhere. "You could have said something! You could have—you should have done something!"

My mother blinked slowly, then looked me in the eye. "It's not that simple, Nathan. Nothing's that simple."

I shook my head violently. "Yes it is. Why not?"

I took a deep breath. "Go on with the freakin' story."

"Project: Rancher needed human subjects to test the process," my mother said. "Your father didn't want them to use convicts, or mental patients, or homeless people."

My eyes widened. "Like that's what they would have used?"

Lucy and Denver exchanged glances again.

"Aw, Jesus Christ." I ran a hand through my never-growing hair. "Fine. So my dad volunteered. Which is, like, fucking ridiculous." I didn't care about swearing in front of my mother at that point. "It's like a bad movie. People don't do that."

"These people did," my mother said. "Your father believed in the potential of the process. Apart from the medical benefits, he knew there was a chance it could help finally decide the war in Vietnam."

I was about to ask how, then remembered the thorns and spikes that sprouted from Brenhurst's goons. "They wanted to make soldiers," I said.

"That's right. Ultimately, it could have meant that fewer people would die." My mother's eyes left the present for a moment. "I was… furious with your father, when he told me. He was home, back from the lab. He'd already done it, days before."

"Why were you so upset? Wasn't he trying to help people?"

She looked a little uncomfortable, but pushed that aside with a tight shake of her head. "He told me after we'd made love, Nathan. We didn't know it then, but we'd conceived you. And I had a pretty good idea that's what had just happened… or could have just happened."

I looked at Denver Colorado, who was silent, listening. I guess his part of the story wasn't up yet.

"So that's why I'm how I am." I felt a little nauseous. "That's why he's like he is." I took a deep breath and let it out in a rush. "So… do I have these little machines in me, too?"

Denver shook his head. "Nope. If you did, you'd be dead right now."

"What?"

My mother held up a hand. "We're getting ahead of things. Your father went back to the desert, back to the lab, about a month later. By then, we knew I was pregnant. One of the reasons he went back was to make sure there weren't any side effects, that you'd be all right."

"Was he already starting to, I don't know, get to be like he is now?"

She seemed to consider that. "Looking back… I think he was. He was distracted. He would fixate on things. His concentration was either very focused, or just shattered. That's how it seemed."

"His senses were getting sharper," I said. I had some idea of how fascinating a little detail could get. A scent, or a rustle in the grass you couldn't see, but could hear. Even the knowledge you were aware of things everyone else missed could be hypnotic.

I couldn't read my mother's expression as she looked at me. Finally, she just nodded and went on. "That last time he left was the last time I saw him. Until this morning."

I threw out a test question. "They told you there was an explosion?"

A deep regret pulled at my mother's face. "No. They told me he'd gone mad. That he'd been violent, attacked several people at the lab, and that he'd been killed in the struggle."

"So you made it all up." I searched myself sympathy for my mother. It wasn't there. I kept seeing my father's crazy-eyed, bearded face.

A bit of defiance bloomed in her. "I did it to protect you, over the years. I didn't want you to think of your father as a madman. I didn't want you to think he'd made such a huge mistake."

She looked at Denver, who nodded in encouragement.

"I came to hate what they were doing out there," she said. "I knew how things were. Any belief I'd had that they'd ever use that technology for the greater good seemed ridiculous, once that happened to Andrew. And when Denver told me Andrew was still alive…"

Denver shifted in his chair. "Ah. Here's my cue." He flashed a nervous smile and licked his lips.

"About two months after Lucy told me he was dead, Andrew showed up in Kirby Lake. Nearly scared the shit out of me. He was… he was pretty much the way you saw him today, I guess. Like a wild man."

I nodded. "You've been, like, taking care of him… hiding him."

Denver shrugged his massive shoulders. "Not all that much. Mostly in the winter, I'll give him shelter if he wants. Thing is, see, he doesn't usually want it. It makes him nervous to be around people."

He shook his head and smiled. "We're too slow. Too blind. His senses—it's like he lives in a whole different world."

My eyes narrowed. "I get it."

He frowned. "I guess you think you do… but you only inherited a fraction of your daddy's talents, kid. You literally don't know the half of it."

I knew that was true.

"Mom."

"Yes, Nathan?"

"You knew all along… that he was up in the mountains around Kirby Lake. That's why we went up there when all this Sovereign stuff started?"

Denver answered. "Actually… no." He gave my mother an apologetic look, his eyebrows high on his forehead. "Andrew didn't want anyone to know he was still alive. He didn't want to… I don't know. I tried to change his mind." Denver looked away from us both for a moment. "He wanted to be dead, far as you were concerned. Maybe he just didn't want to be a bother."

I snorted. "Maybe he shouldn't have, like, fucking experimented on himself, then, you think?"

Denver allowed for that with a nod. "I told Lucy I'd seen him, just for a little bit, before he disappeared into the woods. That was when you were just a baby. I wanted to give her hope."

I looked at my mother. "And you still decided you'd tell me he was dead."

"I didn't want you to think your father was a coward. Unable to face us, with all that had happened to him."

"Is that what you think? You think he was ashamed?" I stood up. I dearly wanted to think differently. I've felt that same isolation, even if it's just a fraction of what he knew. I know what it feels like to be absolutely, profoundly different from everyone else.

I was used to it. I'd had my whole life to live that way. What would it have been like to be a normal person, and then wake up like that?

"You don't get it. Neither one of you do."

I paced back and forth between the living room and the kitchen. I didn't want to be in the house with them any more.

"You don't get it," I said again. I shook my head.

"Thanks for the story."

I opened the front door.

"Nathan, wait," my mother said. I walked out, slammed the door. Of course, I could still hear Denver.

"Let him go, Lucy. It's a lot to take in."

"Fuck you, Denver!" I hollered from the driveway. Maybe if I hadn't waited sixteen years to hear it all. Maybe then, I'd be all smiles.

FORTY-SEVEN

I walked. I thought about going to Mel's, but something kept me going when I came to his house. I didn't want to talk to someone who hadn't been there this morning. I didn't want to have to explain everything. I wanted someone who understood.

I ended up at Romita Park, where I lay down on the damp grass. I stared at the sky and wondered if I should go to Lina's.

I couldn't be sure I'd be allowed to see her. I was basically responsible for putting Mr. and Mrs. Porter's daughter through your basic traumatic experience. Because of me, they were probably going to be involved in a cross-fire of lawsuits between my mother and the Federal government.

Small insects lit on my arms, tasted, and flitted away. The grass tickled the back of my neck, and the small of my back where my tee-shirt rode up.

I stood up, brushed myself off. I was a mess. These were the same clothes I'd had on since I left the house last night to doorbell ditch Byron's house. My shirt and jeans were stained with dirt and sweat and blood. None of that blood was mine. I stank.

I frowned. It didn't matter, did it? I wanted to see Lina, and her parents saw me like this in Kirby Lake. Changing clothes was not worth going back to my mother.

FORTY-EIGHT

It was a long walk. It was late afternoon by the time I was in the right neighborhood and reached Lina's house.

I knocked on the door.

Mister Porter answered. He had reading glasses on, his feet were bare, and his pale blue dress shirt was untucked. His eyes looked tired.

"Hello, sir."

He frowned. "Nate?" He looked over my shoulder, then back at me. "Did you ride your bike?"

I tried to catch Lina's scent. "Um, I walked." He had opened the door just far enough to fit his frame. The house was quiet beyond. "Is… is it all right to see Lina? Is she home?"

Mister Porter regarded me with a curious expression. "You walked."

"Yeah."

He nodded, and seemed to make a decision. "I bet you're hungry." He opened the door and made room for me to come in.

As I stepped inside, he wrinkled his nose. "Son, you're a mess."

"I'm sorry… I haven't had a chance to…"

Tim appeared. "Hello Nathan!" he barked. He grabbed my hand and pumped it up and down. "Six!" He smiled.

"Hi, Tim."

Tim continued to shake my hand for a few seconds, then turned on his heel and went upstairs.

"You've made a friend," Mister Porter said. "He doesn't usually like to touch people."

I smiled tiredly. "I'm glad." I really was. I felt like we had some things in common, in a way. "So, should I wait for Lina down here, or…"

Mister Porter pushed the frames of his reading glasses onto the bridge of his nose. "Tell you what. Lina's taking a nap, and to be perfectly frank, Nate, you're in no condition to see her."

"Oh."

He waved a hand. "No, don't misunderstand me." He touched my shoulder and led me down a short hall off the kitchen. "We've got a bathroom down here. Why don't you get a shower, and I'll see if I can find some clothes for you. You're about Tim's size, more or less."

A shower. Suddenly my whole body burned to be clean. "That… that's really great."

He shrugged and smiled wryly. "Well, like I said, you're a mess, and Lina's mother probably wouldn't have let you in the house if she'd answered the door. By the time you're finished, I'll make sure Lina's up."

I stood in the doorway of the bathroom. "Mr. Porter… you're not upset?"

He looked me square in the eye. "You think you screwed things up?"

"I don't know."

He nodded. "You kids saw some pretty awful things today, right?"

"That's why I wanted to see Lina," I said. "Make sure she's okay."

He kept looking at me. There was a lot of compassion on his face, and something else. Resolve, maybe. Or maybe, if he was angry, it wasn't with me.

I couldn't be sure. I didn't have a whole lot of experience with fathers who weren't crazy animal men.

"Get your shower, Nathan." He closed the bathroom door.

This was the extra, downstairs bathroom, and it was as big as the single one my mother and I shared at our house. The pressure in the pipes was strong, and the water really hot. It was fantastic.

While I was in there, Lina's dad knocked on the door and left some folded clothes on the sink counter top. He scooped my own clothes off the floor and took them with him.

After I finally turned off the water and toweled dry, I dressed in a pair of grey sweatpants and a blue sweatshirt with "UCLA" embroidered across the chest.

A strong, soapy perfume hit my sinuses when I pulled the sweatshirt over my head. My nose wrinkled, and I sneezed. Apparently, the Porters used a different detergent than my mother, and these clothes were freshly washed.

I'd get used to it.

Lina sat with her parents on the big couch in the living room. She lit up when she saw me.

"You walked here..?"

It was so good to see her. Since she left the police station in Kirby Lake that morning, I'd been carrying a heavy unease in my gut. I didn't even realize it was there until the sight of her made it disappear.

"I needed some air."

Mrs. Porter smiled as well, but her eyes seemed as tired as her husband's. "Do you feel better, Nate?"

"I do, thanks." I tugged at the sweatshirt. "Where's Tim? I want to thank him for the clothes."

"He's working on his numbers," Mrs. Porter said. "But he picked those out for you himself."

I was touched by that. I took Lina's hand.

Mister Porter said, "I took the liberty of calling your mother, Nate. To let her know you were okay."

"Thanks," I said, levelly.

There was some strained silence. I wanted to talk to Lina. I didn't know what to say to her with her parents sitting there.

Mister Porter stood up. "We're going into the back yard," he said, as much to Mrs. Porter as to Lina and I. "Catch the sunset."

"Thanks again, Mister and Mrs. Porter," I said.

Lina and I were alone. I sat down next to her and gave her a long hug.

"Are you okay?" Her breath was hot and sweet on my neck.

I sighed. I was worried about her, she was worried about me. That's what it was supposed to be about, I thought.

"I'm better now," I said. Then I told her about Project: Rancher, and Brenhurst, and all the rest.

"This morning," Lina said when I was done. "Do you think that thing Brenhurst had—that box. Do you think it was supposed to kill your dad, too?"

I remembered the look on Brenhurst's face when we all noticed my father was gone.

"Yeah, I think that was the plan. Brenhurst asked my dad if he was ready, right before he pushed the button."

"Ready to rest, he said."

"Yeah." I thought about what Denver had said at the house. "And Denver Colorado told me I'd be dead if I was like my dad, with those little gizmos in him. Instead of, like, naturally different… if that makes sense."

We sat on the couch, leaning into each other. My head was on Lina's shoulder.

"Lina."

"Yeah, baby?"

"It got crazy."

She pecked the top of my head. "Crazier, you mean? And it's not over, huh, what with your mom and my folks going after Brenhurst, and Brenhurst and Byron's folks probably going after you and your mom?"

That wasn't even all of it. How could I live a normal life, now that I knew what I knew? Now that I knew what I was, and how I got that way? I wondered about Brenhurst's agents, and Tyndale Labs, and Project: Rancher. I'd wondered how Byron was, all cut up and in the hospital. I wondered what his parents were thinking, right now.

I felt like I couldn't go home. I felt like the only place I belonged was in Lina's arms. And I couldn't stay with her on the couch forever.

"Yeah," I finally said. "Hey, seriously… are you okay?"

She sighed. "I keep seeing everything over and over again. Did you know I could smell that gun? I could smell it." She shuddered. "I could have done without that. And those poor men, or whatever they were."

I sat up and kissed her gently. "I'm sorry, Lina. Really sorry."

"I know. But what else were we supposed to do?"

I thought about what Byron had said. "Well, for starters, we could have gone right to my mother, instead of treating it like one of Jason's little crime sprees."

"Yeah." She kissed me back. "But we didn't, and you got to meet your dad, for, like, the first time ever. And now you know the truth about stuff, right?"

"Yeah," I sighed. The truth didn't do anything but add more questions. More opportunities to be deceived.

"You hungry?"

Of course I was. Once again, we made sandwiches in her kitchen and tried to be a couple of normal kids in love.

FORTY-NINE

Eventually, Lina drove me home. We noticed Denver's van was gone. Lina didn't come in.

It was about nine o'clock at night. My mother sat at the kitchen table. She looked relieved.

"Nathan. I love you, you know."

I knew it.

"I know, Mom." I stood on the carpet at the edge of the kitchen, arms slack, my balled-up dirty clothes in one hand. "I just… I don't get it, yet. I'm really… angry."

It felt strange. I was used to being persecuted, feeling frustrated, misunderstood, disliked, helpless. This variety of anger was such a proactive emotion… as tired as I was, when I thought about it, when I really felt it, it made me want to do something. Act.

"Angry with me," she said.

I nodded. "And with Brenhurst, and Denver Colorado, and… and with my dad." I sighed, and hated the weepy tremor that shook my chest. "Why'd he take off again, mom? What's the point, now, with everybody knowing everything?"

"I don't know."

"I'm goin' to bed," I said, and left her in the kitchen.

Friday was finally over.

FIFTY

Saturday, I woke with a start from a dream I forgot as soon as I opened my eyes. The smell of blood faded from memory, leaving me confused, and somehow hungry and nauseous at the same time.

I rubbed my eyes. It was eleven. Late. That explained the hunger.

I put together a quick, but large, sandwich in the kitchen. I could see my mother through the window, puttering in the back yard. When she saw me, she put down her shears, took off her gloves, and came inside.

"How did you sleep?"

I grunted. "Not well, I don't think. Bad dreams."

"I can only imagine." She nodded. "Nathan, what happened yesterday… do you need any help? Processing it?"

I raised an eyebrow. "Why? Is there something else you never told me?"

Her face darkened. I could see she was putting her guilt behind her. "I'm talking about what we went through. You saw your father kill someone, Nathan."

"Yeah." I thought about it. Did it bother me? Was I scarred for life? Should I be more freaked out?

"Well?"

I shrugged. "I don't know. How am I supposed to react?" I took my sandwich and sat down at the table. My mother sat down across from me.

"There isn't any 'supposed' about this. That's why I'm asking."

"I don't know." I took a bite and chewed and thought some more. I knew what she meant, after all. Post traumatic stress, or something like that. I thought about the dream that hid just beyond my memory. Was that part of it?

"Well, how's Lina?"

I swallowed. "I think she's okay." I realized I hadn't asked the same question of my mother… and I didn't really care. That was the anger, I guessed.

I asked anyway.

"What about you?"

A shaky smile wavered on her face and her eyes got brighter. "I had… I had a good cry after Denver left, before you got home." She laughed, barely. "I'm not all right. I saw my husband, alive." She touched the corners of her eyes.

"I still feel like he's dead."

A tinge of empathy tickled my conscience before some kind of cold nothing pushed it away. "Because of how he is?" My voice sounded distant to my own ears. My legs twitched.

She nodded. Tears streaked her cheeks. "He's not the man I knew."

I chewed and swallowed slowly. "How do you know?"

She wiped her eyes with a quick swipe of her hand. "Because he's literally not," she said.

There was more than a little anger in her, too. It was easy to forget. "He let himself be changed by those things. He let himself… he let himself lose his mind."

I felt separate from myself. If only she'd told me the truth. I was old enough. I could have known. I gave her the chance, especially over the last two weeks.

I looked down at my sandwich and finished it. I didn't look up until I was done.

"Can we go see Byron today?"

My mother had been staring at nothing. Her focus came back to me.

"Yes. We should."

I knew something was wrong as soon as we rounded the corner of the corridor to Byron's hospital room. Mister Teslowski rushed down the hallway toward me.

"You son of a bitch!"

He took a swing. I arched my back and watched his meaty fist pass in front of my nose. His other fist came up for my stomach. I tensed and took it. It stung.

Two Orange County sheriff's deputies got behind him and held his arms. Where in the hell had they come from? I saw a nurse step out of a patient's room. She kept well away from the rest of us.

Mister Teslowski's face was deep red. His lips pulled away from his teeth. His eyes blazed.

"Where is he, you fucking freak? What have you done with my son? Where is he?"

"I don't know! What's going on?"

My mother said, "What are you doing, attacking my son?"

One of the cops said, "Mister Teslowski. Please calm down."

Teslowski looked over his shoulder and grimaced. His fists unclenched, but the fury on his face remained. "Fine. I'm fine."

The deputies let him go. One of them had a hand on his nightstick.

Teslowski glared at my mother. "Mrs. Freak."

She stiffened. "How dare you..!"

One of the deputies stepped between Teslowski and my mother and me. He spoke quietly and calmly.

"Have you come to see Byron Teslowski?"

I thought that was a ridiculous question. My mother said, "Well, we didn't come to get assaulted, that's for damn sure."

The deputy nodded. "Mister Teslowski's son is not in his room. Would either of you have any idea where he is?"

Not in his room?

"Uh… maybe he took a walk? He heals really fast…"

Mister Teslowski raged. "He did not go for a fucking walk, freak! What do you know?"

The same deputy looked directly at Byron's dad. "Mister Teslowski. Please keep a civil tongue in your mouth. Sir." His partner stepped closer to Teslowski. Their shoulders touched.

My mother said, "Nathan has been with me since last night. How long has Byron been missing?"

The nurse finally joined the party. "We checked on him this afternoon. He ate lunch. That was two hours ago."

The deputy said, "So, the two of you haven't seen Byron, and you don't have any knowledge of where he might be?"

I shook my head. "No. We came here to see him, to check on him."

"All right." He looked at the nurse. "Was Byron able to get up and walk around?"

She nodded curtly. "He was strong enough. The boy's strong as an ox." She gestured to the doorway. "But he had an I.V."

"Couldn't he have taken it out?"

She shrugged. "Well, I suppose he did, didn't he? But we would have seen him leave. My nurses would have seen him. You can't leave this wing without going past the nurses' station."

"Um, officer?" I said.

"Yes."

"Can I, like, go into his room?"

He looked quickly at his partner. Byron's dad had no doubt told them about me. I figured there was nothing to lose. "I might be able to discover something."

The deputy looked at me sharply. He had a small scar across his left cheek.

"How, exactly?"

I looked at my mother. Her eyes blasted a warning. I felt that cold detachment come over me. I looked back at the cop.

"I have your scent, and your partner's." His eyes narrowed. "I would know Mister Teslowski with my eyes closed. The nurse smells like the hospital and some kind of perfume. And I know what Byron smells like. I've known him for years."

"You're a Sovereign, is that right?"

"Freak!" said Byron's dad. The other deputy looked at him and shook his head once.

"Close enough." Now that I knew the truth, I figured Mister Teslowski's label was more accurate.

The cop considered, and then stepped back. "Go ahead. Don't touch anything."

I went into Byron's hospital room. His father and the deputies came after me. "Wait. Please. If it's okay."

The deputies exchanged glances again, then escorted Byron's dad out of the small room.

I closed my eyes, opened my mouth, and sniffed. The hospital air conditioning diluted everything. I hadn't expected that.

The bed still smelled like Byron, though. Unwashed Byron. What about sponge baths, anyway?

The privacy curtain around the bed was pulled back. I put my nose close to it.

Cigar smoke. In a hospital.

Right.

"Does anyone smoke?"

My mother and Mister Teslowski came in, the deputies between them. The nurse brought up the rear and said, "This is a hospital."

"Well, somebody was in here either smoking a cigar, or somebody was in here who had cigar smoke on his clothes. And he brushed against the curtain."

The silent deputy finally spoke. "Kid, you ever think about a career in law enforcement?"

I smiled grimly. "Let me get out of high school first."

"Fair enough. You got anything else?"

I shook my head. "No. Sorry."

The first deputy said, "All right. I need everyone out of the room, please. This is now a crime scene."

After we gave our official statements to the cops, there was no more reason to be there. I'd talked to police officers more in the last two days than in my whole life.

In the car back home, my mother said, "Were you trying to impress people back there, Nathan?"

I scowled. "I was trying to help."

I looked away from her, out the window. I didn't say anything.

Neither did she. We were silent the rest of the way. I felt like the trip home couldn't be too short.

FIFTY-ONE

The phone was ringing when I opened the front door. I jumped on it so I wouldn't have to talk to my mother.

"Hello?"

"Hello, my friend!"

It was Mel. "Hey. What are you doing right now?"

"Calling you. You want to come over, tell me all about your latest adventures? I haven't heard from you for days."

My mother was standing in the kitchen, waiting.

"Yeah, okay. I'll be right there. Later."

"Later!"

I hung up. My mother crossed her arms on her chest.

"I think we should talk."

"I'm going to Mel's."

She stepped up to me. "I'm still your mother, Nathan. I expect you to act like it."

"Likewise." I walked past her and out the door, which I had to struggle not to slam.

The walk to Mel's is a short one. I angrily strode up the hill and down his street.

I knew I was practically having a tantrum. I was allowing myself to be angry… it was easier than thinking, easier than facing everything that had happened since April eighteenth. Certainly, it was easier than getting over it all.

Mel waited for me on his front step. He stood up when he saw me, and concern creased his face.

"What's going on?"

"You don't want to know," I said. I realized I didn't really want to tell him about it. The idea of going through all the details of the last seventy two hours was exhausting. How could he possibly relate?

"Sure I do." He gestured down the street. "C'mon. I'll buy you a MegaSip."

We started walking.

"I'm gonna give you, like, the Reader's Digest version, all right?"

"Sure, whatever."

I kept my eyes forward. "All right."

I pretended to be distracted by a darting sparrow while I gathered it all together.

"So. That Brenhurst guy works for the government, making fake Sovereign. We took Byron up to Kirby Lake to get him away from him. There was a fight. Byron was in the hospital, now he's gone. Lina had a fucking gun pointed at her head. I saw two people die. My father killed one of them. He's still alive—my mother's been lying to me my whole life. I can't stand to look at her."

I kept walking, reluctantly replaying the whole thing in my head. It took me a moment to realize Mel wasn't next to me. I turned around.

He stood about ten feet back, his mouth agape. I couldn't tell if I was supposed to laugh at the look of total bewilderment on his face. I hoped that's what it was. It could have been worse things, like fear, or disgust. He was my best friend, but he hadn't been there. He was still just a normal person. The experience put space between him and me. Between me and everyone.

Once again, I realized I only felt normal with Lina.

He just stared, and not even at me. It pissed me off.

"You gonna wake the fuck up, Mel? Sorry for the dose of real life."

He shook his head and smiled weakly. "Fucking Christ, Nate. I don't even know where to begin."

I looked him in the eye. "Buy me a fucking MegaSip, then, dude."

He reached out and squeezed my shoulder. "That was the deal, I guess." We kept walking.

FIFTY-TWO

We sat on the sidewalk, our backs against the wall of the convenience store, giant slushy drinks in our hands. I also had a bag of beef jerky for fuel.

"What did you mean, fake Sovereign?"

I tore into a strip of jerky. "They have a way of changing people's DNA, or something. Little machines, small enough to go into your blood."

"So your dad's, like, one of these fake Sovereign, then?"

"Yeah." I swallowed the jerky and spit, my phlegm bright red from the syrup in the drink. It made me think of all the blood I'd seen in Kirby Lake. I pushed the images—the smell—down.

"He fucking volunteered for it, way back. Made him crazy—and I got to inherit his messed up genes."

"You think you're gonna go crazy, too?" He said it conversationally, like he was asking if I was going to watch MTV when I got home.

I laughed, bitterly. "Not from that, anyway. He lost it because he couldn't deal with the changes—the better senses, the speed, the reflexes, all that. I was born that way—or at least a watered-down version of it."

"And your mother never said anything about it." Mel shook his head and looked at the ground between his knees. "That's not right."

"Totally. I can't even handle being around her. I can't even be in the same house. I don't even want to be."

Mel sipped his drink. "Why didn't she tell you?"

I sighed. "She thought it was better. She thought he was a coward for running off on us. Plus, as the years went by, I guess she had to think he was dead for real."

Mel nodded. "What do you think?"

"About what?"

"You think he was a coward?"

"Back then, I don't know. I think he knew he'd screwed up. I think he might have been ashamed. Felt guilty." I could relate to feeling guilty just for being myself. Twisted and wrong, but there it was.

"But now… I mean, we all know more about him, and there's me, being the way I am." I frowned. "There's no more reason to run."

Mel sighed and shook his head again. He rubbed the back of his neck. "Sorry, man."

"Yeah."

Mel started to take a sip of his drink and suddenly stopped. "What about Byron? You think Brenhurst came and got him?"

"I don't know," I said. "I haven't even taken that part in, yet, I guess." I considered it. "Y'know, I bet Byron took off on his own."

"Where would he go? He doesn't even drive."

"No, he's got his learner's." I bit off some jerky. "I don't know. It's crazy."

We walked back. A car honked, and Lina's silver Volkswagen Golf zipped into the bike lane ahead of us.

She popped her head out the window and looked over the roof at us. "Hey, handsome! Hey, Mel."

Mel said, "It would have killed you to just make that 'handsomes?'"

"I'm pretty sure it would," Lina said, smiling. "You guys want a ride?"

Mel looked at me. "Nah, you guys go ahead—I'll solo it the rest of the way."

"Later, Mel." I gave my best friend a grateful smile. He threw me a thumbs-up, and I got in the car.

FIFTY-THREE

Lina wore a black shirt and her tartan skirt. She had made herself up; pale skin with dark red lips.

I kissed her. "You're all dolled up."

"I was on my way to see you, big boy." She touched my cheek, smiled, and wiped lipstick off my mouth before she pulled into traffic.

"I needed an excuse not to go home," I said. "Good timing."

"Hm. What's going on? And where do you want to go?"

"I just… I just can't stand being there. I can't stand being around my mother, or in our house, or anything that reminds me I've been living with a person who's been lying to me for the past, like, forever." I took a deep breath and let it out.

"Right." She paused. "So, have you, like, talked to her about it?"

"She felt bad about it for, I don't know, maybe a day?"

"How long do you want her to feel bad about it?"

I was glaring out the window. What she said made me turn and look at her.

"What do you mean?"

Lina kept her eyes on the road.

"Well, she screwed up. She can't fix it. So, now what?"

"I don't know..!" I couldn't tell if Lina was on my side or not. "I just don't know how things can be like they were. I mean, I don't, like… I can't look at her the same way. It's like she lost some of her Mom Privileges."

Lina nodded. "Yeah, I could see that. She did lie to you."

"Totally! For, like, ever!"

We were at a red light. She reached over and put her hand on top of mine. "She thought she was doing the right thing, though, right? Does that count for anything?"

Damn it, I knew that it did. I didn't want it to count, though. I wanted to be angry.

I wanted to be angry.

I said it out loud. "I think I want to be angry at someone. And there's too many choices. My dad's disappeared again. Brenhurst is out of reach. My mother's right here."

Lina smiled. "Like always."

Like always.

I gaped at Lina. I probably looked a lot like Mel had, earlier.

She winked at me, the light changed, and we were on our way again.

I shook my head. "How'd you do that?"

"What?"

I laughed. "Cut through all my bullshit. Like that."

"How? When? We're just talking."

"Now!" I jabbed her in the side, and she squeaked. "You know you did, too!"

She smiled. "You know what my dad said to me this morning?"

"I don't want you to see that Charters kid anymore?" I smiled.

"After that," she laughed. "No—he told me if I wanted to go to art school, I could. That I should do what makes me happy, what I was passionate about."

"Whoa. Why?"

She kept smiling. "He didn't come right out and say it, but I think it was because of what happened at the cabin."

I felt a cold tremor of guilt roil my stomach. "You mean almost getting killed." My voice was sullen with remorse.

She shot me a quick glance. "None of that. My choice to get into all that craziness with you, remember?"

"Yeah..."

"Okay." She nodded firmly. "Anyway, yeah, maybe it was that. I think so, actually."

"Wow."

"Yeah. So who knows what's going to come out of all this? I mean, my dad's letting me do what I want, you and Byron are friends..."

"Byron's gone."

"What? Oh my God!"

"No... I mean, he's not in the hospital. He disappeared. No one knows where he is. Sorry, I didn't, like, say that so right."

"Oh." She let out a breath. "Okay. Where is he?"

"Nobody saw him leave the hospital," I said. "But I think he walked out. He heals fast, and the way he can adapt to the situation, maybe he got, like, super-stealthy or something? Who knows what he can do?"

"Wow. That's crazy." She frowned. "But where would he have gone?"

"That's the thing I can't figure out."

"Man." Lina laughed. "It really is a whole new world."

"Yep."

We drove in silence for a bit. Lina had been circling around the neighborhood. "So," she finally said. "Where did you want to go, anyway?"

I sighed and gave her a sheepish smile. "I guess I need to go home, right?"

She smiled. "I am so gonna be a psychologist." She nodded. "An artist-actress-psychologist."

"Actress-psychologist, now?"

"Well, now that I'm gathering all these big life experiences to, you know, draw on, and whatever."

"Draw on. I get it."

We both laughed. It felt really, really good. I felt like I hadn't laughed for years. If this is what normal was going to be for me, I could handle it, so long as Lina stuck around.

I kept chuckling, randomly, right up until we pulled up to my house. Right up until I saw my mother in the driveway talking to a man in a dark business suit.

FIFTY-FOUR

I saw the dark suit, the nondescript car parked on the curb, and I freaked out. I was out the door before the Lina stopped the car.

"Who is this?" I strode up the driveway.

They turned toward me. I glanced at my mother. She was too calm for this to be a Brenhurst-style situation. I turned my attention to the man.

He wasn't much taller than me, but much stockier. He was bald, but his bushy eyebrows were black.

He stuck out a meaty hand.

"My name is Spencer Croy."

I looked at my mother. She smiled with half her mouth.

I took his hand. He met my eyes steadily as I tested his strength with my grip. He was as strong as I suspected.

"Nate Charters."

He nodded, once, and we disengaged our hands. "Yes, I know. I've been talking with your mother. We were hoping you would be by."

My mother stepped next to me. "Mister Croy is with the Institute, Nathan."

"Institute?" I automatically stepped back. "What 'Institute?' Tyndale? Project: Rancher, maybe?"

Croy's expression soured for an instant. His head moved back and forth, once. Everything he did seemed to use the absolute minimum amount of motion.

"The Donner Institute," he said. "Of Sovereign Studies."

"What?" That was not what I'd been prepared to hear.

My mother said, "That's the compound in Montana."

Croy said, "You might call it a research facility and refuge, all in one. It's the center of the Sovereign nation."

I sniffed him casually. "Are you a Sovereign?" He smelled like soap and... yes, gun oil. Last week, I wouldn't have recognized that smell. I tried to figure out where he was carrying the gun.

"I am," he said levelly.

"Why do you need the gun?"

He squinted at me, and the corners of his mouth twitched. "I am licensed to carry a firearm."

Lina got out of the car. Croy introduced himself. She looked at me uncertainly.

"He's from the Donner Institute," I told her.

"Whoa." She took my hand.

My mother said, "Let's go inside. Mister Croy has some things to tell you."

We went into the house and sat around the kitchen table. Lina was on my left, my mother on my right, and Croy sat across from me. He declined my mother's offer of some water.

"Mister Charters, I'm here on behalf of Dr. William Donner."

I let out a breath that was half gasp, half astounded laugh. "You're kidding me. Donner knows about me?"

"He does," Croy said. "We've known about Project: Rancher for some time. After Declaration Day, we expected something like your adventure in Kirby Lake to happen."

My mother said, "The Institute is interested in helping us with the lawsuit."

"That's right."

I said, "There are Sovereign lawyers?" I knew how stupid it sounded, but what can I say? It was all new territory for me. I tried not to study Croy; I couldn't figure out what his Sovereign ability might be.

That was stupid, too. Byron Teslowski looked as normal as this guy.

Again, Croy flashed the micro-smile. I got the feeling this was a stretch for him. He was trying to be charming.

"There are Sovereign everything," he said.

Okay…

"What do we have to do?"

"I've already given Mrs. Charters the address of our law firm in Los Angeles. We want you to come for a first consultation this week."

"We have an appointment Monday morning," my mother said. She held up a business card.

I took the card and read the names like they would mean something to me. Like I was up on the names of all the Sovereign attorneys.

"Wow." I gave the card to Lina. "That's, like, great, I guess. Thanks."

"Your case has the potential to set an early precedence."

I was jittery, nervous. Lina chewed on her thumb. My mother shifted in her seat every now and then, like anyone would. Croy moved only when necessary. It was like sitting down with one of those animated mannequins at an amusement park.

"That's not the only reason I came in person," he said. "I have information."

We looked at him.

"You don't need to be concerned about your friend Byron. He's with us."

I leaned forward in my seat. "What? Where? Is he all right?"

I finally caught the faintest hint of cigar smoke on Croy's clothes. He wasn't the smoker… but one of his Sovereign friends?

"He's fully recovered. He's at the Institute."

"What's he doing there?" I laughed. "Man. His father must be pissed!"

"His parents don't know," Croy said, "but we will notify them soon."

"When's he coming back?" my mother said.

Croy turned his head toward me, slightly. "He's not. He's with his people."

His people. Right.

After all, Byron was a real Sovereign. Not like me.

"What about his parents? I mean, he's probably better off, don't get me wrong, but you can't just keep him, right?" I looked at my mother. "He's, like, a minor still, right?"

Croy said, "He's Sovereign. And he wants to be with other Sovereign."

I looked at him. His face was stony, but his eyes danced with conviction.

My mother cleared her throat. "There's… there's another thing, Nathan."

I looked at her. She was upset. Not obviously, but there was definitely something she was trying to hold in.

I frowned, sighed. "Okay. What else?"

"About your father, Andrew Charters," Croy said. "You might want to know the rest of his story."

FIFTY-FIVE

I blinked.

"How..?"

"As I said, we've known about Project: Rancher for some time. We discovered your father about six years ago."

Donner and the Sovereign people were active that long ago? I wanted to ask about that, but I didn't want to interrupt Croy's story. So I just nodded.

"You might not know that your father has had a great deal of difficulty adjusting to his abilities," he said.

I nodded. "The world's too slow," I said. "And he remembers what it's like to be human."

"That's exactly correct." Croy's eyes bored into me. "When we found him, his humanity was almost completely submerged. He was like an animal."

Next to me, my mother's breathing became shallow and quick.

"We brought him to one of our sanctuaries, and tried to help," Croy said. "That's when we discovered the truth of his nature, and made the connection with Project: Rancher. Once we knew he had been given the augmentation regimen, we also knew he carried the fail-safes."

"Fail-safes..?"

"The same technique that changed his genetic structure," Croy said, "could be used to kill him."

I visualized Brenhurst's agent, dissolving in a cloud of gore. He was taken apart from the inside… like his own cells grew teeth.

"You… you guys fixed him."

"We have an individual who is able to neutralize the fail-safe factor."

"So, is that where my dad is now? Is he at the Institute with Byron?"

Croy's head moved. "No. Mr. Charters prefers to live in the wilderness. He's out there, now."

I looked at my mother. Her eyes were wet and her face was red. She stared at a spot on the table top.

I reached under the table. She clutched my hand.

I said to Croy, "I thought he ran away. Again."

"I believe your father knew the immediate danger to you and your mother and Ms. Porter was passed. Since he's legally dead, it would have been challenging to explain himself to the authorities when they arrived."

My father hadn't seemed capable of that kind of planning. He acted like a crazy person.

I remembered what Brenhurst had said to him. "You're still in there."

"Comes and goes," my father had replied.

A little laugh broke from my lips. I felt like I would float off the chair.

"I really thought he'd cut out. I thought he'd just run away again."

Croy's iron gaze finally broke away from me. He reached into his lapel pocket. "It's interesting that you should say that," he said. He handed me a folded piece of paper.

I let go of my mother's hand and took it from him. As soon as I did, I knew it was from my father. It was smudged with dirt from his hands. It smelled like soil and sweat and blood.

I breathed it in.

I unfolded it.

His writing was a jagged, hasty scrawl, slanted and uneven, but I could read it.

I didn't even care that Croy was sitting right there. I started to cry, shallow and quiet. I don't think I could have stopped if I'd wanted to.

My mother's hand came away from mine and she touched me on the shoulder. "What does it say, Nathan?"

I handed the paper to her and wiped my eyes. I sniffed loudly. The tears still came. I could barely see.

My mother read his words out loud.

"Dear Nate."

I was close to blubbering. Everything that happened in the last few weeks… everything that had happened, ever… it all washed out of me. I felt my anger and my sadness and my frustration and confusion and everything that had made me who I was for the first sixteen years of my life rushing out, pouring out, leaving me empty. Leaving me ready for whatever I decided to put back in.

"Brave men run," my mother read the short note, "in my family."

The End

February 10, 2004 – September 2, 2005

Acknowledgements

Thanks to Geoff, David, Portia, Kris, Stacee, Mike, Cathy, Terry, Gus, Dave, Sean, Paul, and Karen for helping flesh out the kids and teachers of *Brave Men Run.* You're all in there, in whole or in part, along with more than a few others, and always in my fond memories.

Also thanks to Jan McGee of the Big Bear Grizzly for prompt and gracious research assistance.

Finally, much appreciation for Paul Story of dreamwords.com for the unsolicited extra set of eyes, and to Evo Terra and Chris Miller of podiobooks.com for giving me an audience.

About the Author

Matthew Wayne Selznick lives with his wife and several pets in the High Desert of Southern California. Find Matt on the Internet at mattselznick.com, where you can learn more about this book, the Sovereign Era, and all of his other writing, musical, and new media endeavors.

PLAYING FOR KEEPS

The shining metropolis of Seventh City is the birthplace of super powers. The First Wave heroes are jerks, but they have the best gifts: flight, super strength, telepathy, genius, fire. The Third Wavers are stuck with the leftovers: the ability to instantly make someone sober, the power to smell the past, the grace to carry a tray and never drop its contents, the power to produce high-powered excrement blasts, absolute control… over elevators.

Bar owner Keepsie Branson is a Third Waver with a power that prevents anything in her possession from being stolen. Keepsie and her friends just aren't powerful enough to make a difference… at least that's what they've always been told. But when the villain Doodad slips Keepsie a mysterious metal sphere, the Third Wavers become caught in the middle of a battle between the egotistical heroes and the manipulative villains.

As Seventh City begins to melt down, it's hard to tell the good guys from the bad, and even harder to tell who may become the *true* heroes.

A SUPERHERO NOVEL BY

MUR LAFFERTY

THE BEST FICTION FROM ALL GENRES...

WWW.SWARMPRESS.COM

SENTINELS
WHEN STRIKES THE WARLORD

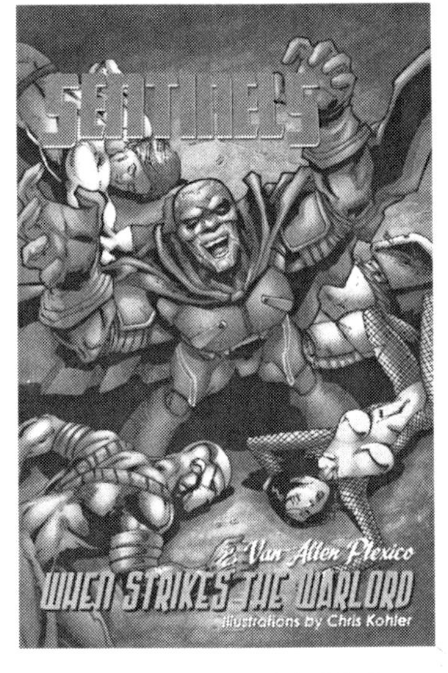

The power-mad Warlord stands poised to conqueror—or destroy!—the universe itself. Can anyone stand in his way?

Enter the **SENTINELS**.

College student Lyn Li...
Brilliant inventor and smart-alec Esro Brachis...
Beloved hero Ultraa...
Flamboyant showman Damon Sinclair...
And mysterious alien powerhouse Vanadium.

When at last they clash atop the Warlord's floating city, can the world itself survive?

ISBN: 1-934861-06-5

SENTINELS
A DISTANT STAR

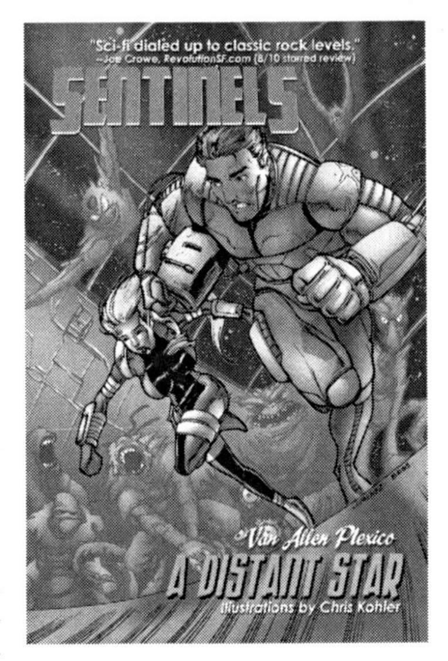

After helping to save the world, all Esro Brachis wanted was a little peace and quiet.

Then the giant robot attacked. And the alien warships landed in his back yard. And then things got really crazy.

Now Esro finds himself hurled halfway across the galaxy. At least he has a beautiful alien warrior woman at his side—if only she didn't want to kill him!

Sentinels: A Distant Star continues the journey and the excitement in a bigger, bolder adventure, with all your favorite heroes and villains from the first book back for more... and many new wonders to encounter!

ISBN: 1-934861-07-3

THE BEST FICTION FROM ALL GENRES...

WWW.SWARMPRESS.COM

Printed in the United States
132238LV00006B/32/P